Jackie's Secret Life: Part 3
The Tangled Web We Weave

By Anita Jefferson

Jackie's Secret Life: Part 3
The Tangled Web We Weave

Copyright @ 2020 by Anita Jefferson

Printed in the United States of America
US Copyright Office
101 Independence Ave. S.E.
Washington, D.C. 20559-6000

Author: Anita Jefferson
Editor: Anjeanette Alexander
Publisher: Kingdom News Today Publication Services

ISBN 978-1735362014

This story is based on fiction and not written or based on factual information about any particular person, place or thing.

Dedication

First, giving honor to God who is the head of my life.

This book is dedicated to all

My Jackie's Secret Life Fans.
Next, to my family and friends.

This book is in memory of the best husband
a woman could ever have
Dwayne Abney
December 23, 1969-August 10, 2018
"Dwayne, you are truly missed."

Table of Contents

SHE'S HERE

"Congratulations, it's a girl!" Dr. Paul Marshall announced as he left the delivery room. Good. Now Jackie and her friends could have some alone time with the happy, but exhausted mother-to-be, Shonda. Besides, she knew her girl well. Surrounded by her girls and her baby daddy, Shonda wouldn't have it any other way.

All of the ladies hugged Shonda as they each cried out.

Jackie said, "What a beautiful, little princess!"

Peace responded next. "She's as pretty as her mom."

"She's so cute," Lisa said.

"Oh my God! What a blessing!" Nikki said.

As Jackie scanned the room, she could see the truth in each of them.

Peace was smiling on the outside, yet crying on the inside: Why not her? Then Lisa, with her fake smile, was still fuming over all that had happened. Finally, Nikki was extremely happy with all that's going on because she's not the center of the drama.

Then the man in the middle of it all, her baby daddy, sat with tears running down his face. He praised God and thanked Him for such a beautiful, healthy baby girl.

Thirty minutes later, Dr. Paul Marshall walked back in. Jackie noticed that he looked better. He recently lost 180 pounds since he and his wife had just divorced.

Dr. Marshall said, "Excuse me, ladies. I know that you are usually in control of everything that goes on in Sterny. However, I'm in control today and as much as this saddens me, I must ask you ladies to leave now. Mommy and daughter need their rest."

The ladies hugged their friend and reluctantly followed Dr. Marshall's instruction. They couldn't resist the temptation of giving the doctor a flirtatious farewell. Jackie wasn't the only one to appreciate how fine he had gotten.

Nikki looked Dr. Marshall up and down as she said, "Sure, Doc. We'll leave peacefully if you are coming with us."

Dr. Marshall said, "Well, Nikki Stewart. That sounds great, but I must take a raincheck. I have three other women here who are ready to deliver at any time, and I need to be here to assist them."

Then Nikki walked over to him and slightly kissed him on the lips. She said, "Boo, you don't know what you are missing."

Jackie glided over to Dr. Marshall. She rubbed his chest and seductively swayed her hips as she exited the room, with Peace following not too far behind. Peace rubbed his cheek with her index finger as she giggled her way out the door.

Finally, Lisa was the last to leave. She grabbed his hands and replied, "Doc, I'll be praying for you."

Shonda turned towards Dr. Marshall, smiled, and then shook her head. "Dr. Marshall, please ignore my friends. They mean well."

"Don't worry, Shonda. I heard about you and your crew. They're fine." He checked the monitor beside her bed before he rested his hand on her shoulder. "Now enough about them. How are you doing?" He gestured towards the right of her. "I see baby and daddy are doing just fine."

A yawn answered his question first before she could get her words out. "I am doing just fine, Dr. Marshall. Just a little tired."

Dr. Marshall said, "Well, I figured that much. That's why I asked the girls to leave before the next group entered the room."

Shonda smiled and said, "You are correct, Doc. They are on their way here now."

Little did she know about what was happening next.

———————————

Jackie and the girls were laughing about what just happened when the elevator door opened. Out stepped the Smith family—Mama and Papa Smith with their son, Richard and his wife, Velma Smith close behind them.

Jackie said, "Hello, everyone. How is everyone doing?"

Peace jumped in the conversation before anyone got a chance to respond. "Richard, the baby is so beautiful. She reminds me of you."

"Thanks, Peace. That's so sweet of you to say," Richard said.

Jackie said, "Papa Smith, how are you doing? Are you excited to be a grandpa, finally?"

Papa Smith wrapped his arms around her. "Jackie, what are you talking about? I'm already a grandpa. You got my three girls, remember?"

Jackie hugged him tighter and kissed him on the cheek. "Aw, Papa Smith! That's why I love you so much."

Velma cleared her throat. "Come on, everyone. Let's see OUR new addition to the family."

She grabbed Richard's hands. "Hubby, are you ready?"

Richard said, "Yes, wifey." He turned toward Jackie and her crew with a curt response. "Bye, ladies."

The ladies entered the elevator and when the door closed, they all laughed.

Lisa said, "Jackie, what was that all about?"

"I have no idea. 'Hubby, are you ready?' Get serious, bitch. We don't want your damn husband," Jackie said.

Peace smirked. "No, Jackie. That wasn't for us. Get it straight. That was for you and only you, my dear."

Jackie's mouth was wide open in fake surprise. "Peace! Why me?"

Peace said, "Because everyone knows that Richie still loves him some Jackie."

They all laughed. The ladies reached the main lobby where they said their goodbyes before getting into their separate cars. Jackie then went home and reminisced on the past year. So many events happened in each of their lives.

How did they get here?

TWO DAYS BEFORE THE RANCH

It's morning time at Sam & Peace's House. Peace stretched her arms out wide as she sat up in her king-sized bed.

Sam said, "Good morning, dear."

Peace said, "Good morning. What time is it?"

"It's about 7:30a.m."

Peace checked the clock on the night stand. "Oh my God, Sam! Why didn't you wake me up?"

He gave her a forehead kiss and said, "Because I absolutely love watching you sleep." He played in her hair and brushed his lips against hers. "Also, I was thinking about our trip to the ranch. Since everyone is so tired and the ranch is about a six hours' drive, why don't we charter a coach bus for everyone to get there?"

Sam's idea jolted Peace wide awake now. She pushed back the covers and searched for her robe. Sam quickly emerged from behind the bedroom door and placed it in her hand.

He continued to speak. "We can meet at E's Place and board the bus there. This way, we will have a driver, and we can relax and drink. We can order the food and drinks from Eric and take them with us on the bus. It will be fun."

Peace said, "Oh, honey. I feel you, but what is this really about?"

Sam laughed. "Baby, you know me so well. Yes, there is a hidden agenda. Tim feels that it would be a great opportunity to develop a campaign strategy with all of our closest friends."

He and Peace rinsed out the toothpaste from their mouths in front of their double vanity sink. They crossed over each other and reached for the his and hers hand towels.

Peace said, "Will Tim be joining us?"

"I believe so because I invited him." Sam took the corner of his towel and wiped the corner of her lip. He cupped her face in his hands. "He had a few concerns because it seemed like mostly couples were going. He did not want to feel like a third wheel."

Peace leaned back with concern. "Oh, Sam. I hope you informed him that no one is walking around all booed up other than that sinner, Nikki. She and Eric are usually kissing all over each other like horny teenagers."

Sam laughed hysterically and said, "Peace, I need you be nice to Nikki. She has particularly good connections that we need, and besides, she is incredibly good to you."

Peace planted her hands on her waist and said, "I still do not trust her. She is a sneaky, little bitch. But I will do it only because I love you, and I know she is not that bad."

They both laughed before getting into the shower together.

GETTING READY

After getting dressed, Peace started her day as usual with a phone call to her best friend, Jackie.

Her receptionist, Kelly, answered the phone. "Good morning, Jackie Lewis' office."

"Good morning. May I speak with Jackie, please?" she said.

Kelly's excitement flowed through the receiver. She said, "Good morning, Mrs. Evans. Congratulations on your husband running for mayor. You have my support. I'm so happy for you."

Peace said, "Thank you, Kelly."

"Hold on, I will get Ms. Lewis for you," Kelly placed the call on hold as she dialed Jackie's extension.

Kelly said, "Ms. Lewis, I have Mrs. Evans on line one."

"Thanks, Kelly. Put the phone call through," Jackie said.

Once the call connected, Jackie cradled the phone between her ear and shoulder. "Good morning, sunshine. Why are you calling me almost two hours late?"

Peace replied, "Jackie, are you minding my personal business with me and my husband?"

"Yes, Peace, I am," Jackie said.

"Well, Ms. Nosy Body, if you must know, my husband did not wake me up on time today. He sat in his reclining chair and watched me sleep. He used to do that when we were in college," Peace said.

"Aw, that so sweet. What did he want?" Jackie asked.

Peace said, "Jackie, you know my husband as well as I do. But this time, it was about us. He wants to order a coach bus to get to the ranch this weekend, so no one would have to drive."

Jackie began dancing in her chair. "Hey now! We can really start the party early. Peace, that is great news. Where will the bus pick us up?"

Peace said, "We were thinking at E's Place."

Jackie clapped her hands. She said, "Perfect location. Have you sent out that information yet?"

"No, I will do that this morning. It will have to be via text message, so we will know what size bus to get. I'll do that once I get to my office. Jackie, are you bringing Sexy Chocolate?" Peace asked.

Jackie said, "Believe it or not, I'm not sure what's going on with Barry. I believe that he may have been intimidated by Stanley Lewis."

What Jackie just said surprised Peace big time. "What...Stanley Lewis?"

Jackie said, "Yes, Peace. He was being very arrogant that night. Please let me know what I can do to help you. I'm going to bring a case of Chambolle Musigny Grand Cru because we have a lot to celebrate."

Peace was totally against Jackie's suggestion. Her earrings flapped against the edge of her face as she shook her head. She said, "Not that wine. It is too expensive. A case is over $19,000 dollars."

Jackie said, "Please, Peace. I won it in the divorce from Stanley. I am going to call Barry and see if he's coming with us. Then maybe he'll get some."

They both laughed. Peace said, "Jackie, you are crazy. If you and the girls can call your people to see who wants to take the bus Friday, that would be a big help."

Jackie said, "Sure, that will be no problem. We will touch bases within two or three hours. Is that enough time?"

Peace said, "You know that if you are spending money, there is no such thing as a short notice. Only extra cash."

Jackie giggled in agreement as they ended the call.

THE CALLS

Peace called the Taylors first. "Good morning, First Lady Lisa. My husband has decided to rent a coach bus to get us to and from the ranch. I was wondering if you and Pastor Mark would like to join us."

Lisa said, "Hey Peace. I believe that would be great. We are both so tired. We were just talking about getting a car to come up there. These last couple of weeks have been so overwhelming. With our wedding and your party, I can use a small break."

There was a brief silence on the line. She said, "Hold on. Mark is right here."

Peace listened quietly as Lisa placed her hand over the phone. She said to Mark, "Sam decided to order a bus to get us to the ranch. Peace would like to know if we are interested in joining them."

Mark said, "Tell her we would love to, but we also have Deacon Jerry Rhodes. Maybe our son, Todd, if he is coming."

Lisa moved her hand and said to Peace, "We're in, but Deacon Jerry and Todd will be riding with us."

Peace said, "Tell Pastor that is why we are calling. Sam does not want anyone to drive so that would be fine. We are going to leave from E's Place at about 10a.m."

"Okay, Peace. Thank you so much for thinking of us. We will see you Friday," Lisa said.

When the call ended, she turned to Mark. "It is not a problem. Does Shonda know that you invited Jerry?"

He said, "What! I did not know that I needed her permission to invite my friend to the ranch. He was a good boy and gave a $500 donation to one of her charities, so I do not think it will be a problem."

Mark stopped talking. Lisa's arms distracted him. He raised each one and checked for excess weight. He said, "Now, did you go to the gym this morning?"

Lisa said, "No. I am starting Monday."

He said, "I'm not going to tell you anymore. I will not have a fat ass wife walking around with me. You better be up on Monday. This is your last warning. Do you hear me?"

Lisa said, "Yes, Mark. I hear you."

Mark said, "I'm leaving now. Make sure you wear what I have laid out for you tonight for bible class. Your other clothes look too damn cheap. It looks like you have been shopping at TJ Maxx or Walmart."

Lisa wondered how he could build up a congregation, but tear down his wife. She said, "Ok, will do. Bye."

As he was leaving, Lisa looked out the window and thought to herself if he was worth it. The new Tom Ford's in her closet answered for her. Yes, money can make her happy.

Lisa said, "Hey Shonda. Have you spoken to Peace yet?"

"No, not today," she said.

Lisa said, "Well, she will be calling in a minute to speak with you about the bus."

"What bus?" Shonda asked.

Lisa said, "Sam has decided to rent a coach bus to get us to the ranch. She called to see if we wanted to ride with them. I also found out that my husband invited Deacon Jerry Rhodes, and I didn't know if you planned on bringing him or London."

Shonda said, "I am so glad you informed me of that. Jerry will be my date then. "

Shonda's caller ID flashed across the phone's screen. "Oh Lisa, speak of the devil. It's Peace on my other line. I will call you later."

She clicked over to the other line. "How are you, dear?

Peace said, "Hey Shonda. Sam and I want to know if you would like to ride the coach bus with us to the ranch on Friday."

Shonda said, "Yes, I would. I can cancel my rental car now. Tell Sam thanks to both of you."

Peace said, "Deacon is coming. Do you mind sharing a cabin with the Taylors and the Deacon?"

Shonda said, "No, I don't mind. Lisa and Mark are cool cabinmates. Wait a minute. Did you invite London?"

"Yes. He's bringing the lady that came to the party with him. Will that be a problem?" Peace asked.

Shonda said, "No. But as for the Deacon, let Mark know this was your idea. I do not need any of his wise-cracking jokes."

Peace smiled. "Okay, cool."

Shonda knew she shouldn't have slept with London. He made her SICK. She needed to get him straight before this bus ride takes place.

SHONDA CALLS LONDON

London smiled at the name on his caller ID. He said, "Hey, beautiful. I knew you would be calling for some more of me."

"Big head, please. This is Shonda," she said.

London said, "I know who I'm speaking with. Are you ready for our next sex around the bed? You know you liked that. We started at the top and did it all around the bed."

"Do not flatter yourself, London. I just spoke with Peace, and I understand that you are bringing a date on the ranch trip,' Shonda said.

"Well, I did RSVP for two, but you can persuade me to come as your date if you are going to let me hit that again," he said.

She couldn't stand how London was so full of himself. The sex wasn't all that. Well, it did make her hit some high notes. Still, he needed to check his ego.

Shonda said, "That is not going to happen. I will be attending with Jerry."

London said, "You and I both know that he can't turn you on like I do."

She said, "It's not all about sex. Deacon Rhodes is a very well-respected man in our community."

"Yeah, yeah, yeah. People only say things like that when they have a little dick, Shonda," he said.

Shonda wanted to throw her phone across the room. She said, "You are so ignorant! I have no idea how big or small his penis is. Just in case you had not noticed, I was a virgin."

As soon as she said it, Shonda regretted sharing that truth with him.

London said, "YESSSSS! I knew it! I knew that I busted your cherry. You know what they say, Shonda. You will always love your first."

Shonda screamed. "London, what is wrong with you! Have fun with your black bimbo, Diane. I'll be with a real man."

Unfazed by her frustration, London said, "But you will be thinking of me. I will see you there."

Shonda couldn't stand him, but she couldn't deny that she did have some feelings for him. She said, "Will you be riding the bus with us?"

He said, "What a party bus! Hell, yes. We are in." He chuckled out loud. "You just keep your hands and eyes on your side of the room. Jealousy doesn't look good on you. It would only expose you to your friends and that old ass cockroach that I have tapped that ass already."

Shonda hung up the phone and screamed, "I hate London Foster! I can't believe that I gave him some. What was I thinking?"

22

A text came across her phone: *Wear something sexy, so I can rip it off you again. You know that I am good for it.*

Shonda hit the delete button. If only it would delete London permanently from her heart.

JACKIE & BARRY

"Damn, Jackie. I mean...Hello, Ms. Lewis. What did I do to deserve this honor?" Dr. Barry Scott said.

Jackie said, "I wanted to know if you will be attending the ranch trip this weekend."

"Are you asking me to join you as your date?" he asked.

"Perhaps, I am. Is that a yes?" she said.

He laughed. "You are something else. Tell me this. Do you want me to piss off Dr. Richard Smith or your ex-husband?"

She said, "Heavens, NO! Why would you ask me something like that?"

Barry cleared his throat and paused for a moment. Jackie couldn't understand his hesitation. She racked her brain to remember if it were something she said or did. The continued silence unsettled her.

Jackie said, "Barry, if I did or said something to offend you, I truly apologize. I really do—"

Barry said, "If I may be honest with you. . ."

"Yes, please do," Jackie said.

He continued. "On the night of Peace's party, I had your phone in my pocket. I got about a mile away before I discovered it. When I got to your house to return it, I saw Richard at your door."

Jackie could feel the shift from his casual tone to one of anger. She didn't know that he saw Richie at her door.

Barry said, "So, I just kept driving. Then you called me about an hour later to ask me about your phone. I was still out driving around steaming mad. So, I just left it in your mailbox."

He paused again.

Jackie said, "Oh my God, Barry! I am so sorry about that."

Barry said, "I was not going to say anything, but I must ask you now, "Is there anything still between you and Richard?"

The question hovered over them like an unwelcomed guest.

Jackie said, "Let me be clear. I do not want Richard. It has been over."

Barry said, "Okay, so why was he at your home that night? You two looked a little bit too close for comfort."

She explained, "He wanted to see if I was okay after my ex-husband came in all cocky acting. That is all. He tried calling me before going to the hospital, but my phone died."

Oh no, there was that silence again. Jackie was not the type to give up so easily. She said, "Do you forgive me? No matter what, Richard and I are just friends."

He sighed. "Jackie, I wish you were not so damn fine. Yes, I would love to go with you this weekend if you are driving." Barry had no choice to concede to a beautiful woman who had already captured his heart.

She said, "Great! Sam and Peace ordered a charter bus. It will pick us up at E's Place at 10a.m."

"You are something else, Jackie," Barry said.

SAM CALLS ERIC

"Good afternoon, E's Place. How may I help you?" Yolanda, the bartender, said.

"Good afternoon, this is Sam Evans. May I please speak with Eric?"

She said, "Hold on, please."

Yolanda immediately got Eric on the phone. She said, "Mr. Evans is on line one."

Eric said, "Thank you, Yolanda." He said to Sam, "Hey, Mr. Mayor! What is going on?"

Sam said, "A lot. Look, my wife and I have decided to get a coach bus to drive all of us up to the ranch on Friday. Can we all meet up at your restaurant and possibly even leave our cars there, if needed."

Eric said, "Man, you don't know how happy you just made me. Boy, all week I have been dreading the drive up there. I have not recouped from the surprise wedding, Peace's party, your announcement for candidacy for mayor, and most of all, Stanley's and London's dates for the event."

Sam laughed and said, "It has been a crazy month."

Eric said, "Hold on, Sam. Someone's knocking at my door, man." He yelled. "Who is it?"

A deep voice spoke through the door. "It is your money man."

Eric laughed. "Sam, speak of the devil. It's London."

"Let him know that he and his date are also invited to join us on the bus there," Sam said.

Eric said, "Sam and his wife have ordered a coach bus for Friday's drive to the ranch."

London said, "Shonda informed me."

"Shonda!" Eric and Sam shouted at the same time.

Eric said, "Wait, wait. . . London, what is going on with you and her?"

"Man, nothing. Peace called her, and she called me. That is all," he said.

Nikki entered the room. Eric and London greeted her. Then she said to Eric, "Who are you on the phone with?"

"Nosy, if you must know, it's Sam. Baby, they have ordered us a coach bus so that no one will have to drive to the ranch Friday. You are so lucky. You are off the hook from driving."

London laughed at Nikki's expression.

"Excuse me, Eric. I was not driving you anywhere," Nikki said.

Sam said, "Let her know that we are also ordering food and drinks from your place for the ride. This should be for about 50 people. Send me an invoice so that I can get you a check before we leave."

Eric told Nikki what Sam said. "Not a problem. I will send him the bill," she said.

Sam said, "I'll see you all Friday. We should be taking off by 10a.m., hopefully, if everyone is on time."

Eric said, "Man, thanks again for the bus ride. I really needed that."

"No problem. I honestly believe we all needed it this time," Sam said as he hung up the phone.

A call from Stanley Lewis comes through as soon as Sam hung up the phone. He said, "What's going on?"

"Mayor Samuel Evans, how are you?" Stanley said.

"Busy as hell, Stanley. Just trying to wrap up this weekend so that I can begin campaigning full force," Sam said.

"That is the reason why I am calling. Tara and I will be at the ranch this weekend as well, if that's okay," Stanley said.

Sam said, "Stanley, man. We FRAT forever, the more the merrier. Your ex-wife will be there, though. I am not sure if she will have a date. But please come. It will make for an interesting weekend."

Stanley said, "When I found out that my wife had been cheating on me for more than half of our marriage, I was devastated. I just wanted out, so I gave her everything—the house, the business, the money, my dignity—everything. But she won't take my life anymore. I'm keeping my friends, and if it makes her uncomfortable, oh, well."

Sam said, "Women are more secretive than men. Peace never told me about none of that. She had to know because they tell each other everything. Come and enjoy the weekend. You know how we do it." Sam and Stanley did their frat call. Stanley thanked him for understanding as they ended their conversation.

JACKIE CALLS NIKKI & PEACE

Nikki said, "What is going on, Jackie?"

Jackie said, "Did Peace call you or Eric about the chartered bus to the ranch?"

"Yes, Jackie. We will be there with the food and drinks for the ride," she said.

"You know what I was thinking, Nikki? Let's put some games together for the ride and make it a fun time that we will be talking about for years to come," Jackie said.

Nikki said, "That is a good idea. I have a few ideas already. Are you bringing Sexy Chocolate?"

Jackie said, "Yes. Why?"

"I am simply curious. That is all. Bye, girl," she said.

"Bye, Nikki," Jackie said as she hung up the phone.

Later on that day, she and Peace discussed their progress in setting up the trip.

Jackie said, "I believe we are all in. Everyone has confirmed. We all are so happy that you guys are reserving a bus."

Peace said, "I did not realize that so much had happened in the last two weeks. Sam came up with a good plan. Thank you so much for your help. I will talk to you later."

The ladies wished each other a good evening.

NIKKI PREPARES FOR THE BUS TRIP

At E's Place, Nikki was reviewing the catering order with Hector and his staff. She managed her team with an inflexible expectation for excellence. Everything had to be done correctly.

She spoke her directives without stopping to take a breath. "Hector, please make sure all the sandwiches are labeled properly. I do not need no vegan messing around and eating a ham and cheese sandwich. I don't want to hurt anyone. And Hector, please make sure that all the condiments are on the side including the lettuce, tomatoes, and onions, and Hector, please make sure that the bread is extra fresh and that we have an assortment. Hector, did your staff put the labels on all the water bottles that we are taking with us?"

Hector replied to his staff quietly, "Puta quiero que salga llamando a mi nombre." His staff giggled.

Nikki said, "Hector, what did you say about me?"

He replied, "Nothing, Ms. Nikki. You the boss."

She said, "Maria, what did he say?"

"He says only jokes. He wishes this b would quit calling his name," Maria said.

Nikki said, "Hector, I am sorry. I just want it done right."

"Madame Nikki, do me always do great job?" he said.

"Yes, you do," Nikki answered.

He said, "Ok, then, Ms. Nikki. Bye, bye. See you Monday."

Nikki said, "Bye, Hector."

Before she walked out of the kitchen, he asked, "Ms. Nikki, who is the boss when E is not here?"

Nikki answered, "You are."

"Ok, Ms. Nikki. E is not here right now. I got this," Hector said.

Nikki laughed as he escorted her out of the kitchen.

HEADED TO THE BUS

Sam was dressed and ready to go. They should have left a long time ago. He stared at his watch in frustration.

He said, "Come on, honey. It would be a shame that the people who ordered the bus and organized this trip are the last ones on the bus. Then you know we will have the worst seats on the bus."

Peace said, "Okay, okay, Sam. Just give me a few more minutes."

He said, "We don't have time, Peace. We will be next to the bathrooms. And you know the rules of the bus ride are that the seats you are in going to the destination will be the same seats you sit in coming back."

Peace said, "I am coming as fast as I can. I have just a few more items to get."

Sam said, "Hurry up."

"Why, Sam? Are we picking up the girls?"

"No, Peace. The girls are not coming. You know that."

She finally stood in front of him, dressed and ready to go. "Here I am. I told you I would be right down." Peace gave him a kiss.

He said, "Do not think that this little kiss would make it all better, Peace."

"That is First Lady Peace to you, Sam." They both laughed as they walked out of the door.

Dr. Barry Scott blew his car horn. Jackie still hadn't come out. Five minutes later, he rang her doorbell. He could hear Jackie telling him that she was coming.

She opened the front door and said, "Hey there, Doctor."

He said, "Jackie, I thought you were ready."

"My daughters called to say they were not coming with us," she explained.

Barry said, "Ah, does that mean I have you all to myself?"

Jackie smiled.

He said, "Now where are your bags? I do not want to be the last couple on the bus. We'll mess around and get stuck by the bathroom."

Lisa said, "Are you ready yet?"

"I will be right down," Mark said.

Lisa called out to her son. "Todd, Oh Todd, where are you? Let's go."

"Mom, I told you. Grandma is on her way to pick me up. I am not going. We have sectionals going on in wrestling," he said.

"When did you start wrestling?" she asked.

"Dad, please do something with your wife. She is not listening again," Todd said to Mark, but he didn't respond.

"Mom, Dad has been to several tournaments. Where have you been? Where do you think I am when I am not at church on some Sundays? Geesh!" Todd said.

Mark came downstairs and kissed Todd on the forehead. He said, "Good luck, dude. Pin him in the first round. Remember, second place is still losing, and we are not LOSERS. "

He said, "Got it, Dad. Do something about her. She's a little dingy sometime."

Lisa said, "I am still your mother."

"Yeah, yeah, Mom. Have fun," Todd said.

Mark laughed, "Are you ready, Lisa?"

"Yes, let's go. We don't want to be sitting by the bathroom," Lisa said.

———————————

Velma called Richard. She said, "What is your ETA? We should have left ten minutes ago."

Richard said, "Hello to you as well. I am about ten minutes away."

"The driver is here already to pick us up," she said.

"Ok, honey. I had to make my final rounds. I am so sorry that I am a thorough doctor. Did you finish packing my bag for me?" he asked.

She said, "Yes, I did. You do realize that you do not have a lot of casual clothes. I must go shopping for you when we get home."

Richard said, "Who cares? I am five minutes away." He finally pulled up and retrieved their items out of the house and proceeded to the limo.

Velma said, "I really hope we do not have to sit next to the restroom."

Diane pulled up and blew the horn for London. She popped open the trunk. He ran out and put his bag into her truck.

While driving, she asked, "Be honest with me. Are you using me to make your ex-girlfriend jealous?"

He cleared his throat and said, "What would make you say that?"

"You do not act as if you are genuinely interested in me. Look, I enjoy hanging out with you, but if you are not that into me and using me to get to Shonda, that's fine. I just need to know," she said.

London said, "Is it that obvious? It did not start out that way with you for me. You are super fine and smart as hell. That is usually the type of chick that I am in to."

She said, "So what's the problem?"

He drew in a deep breath and said, "I am in love with Shonda, and unfortunately, I waited too long to express my feelings for her. Now this church dude creeped in. What I did not want to do was to lead you on. That is why I did not pursue you by trying to sex you all up."

He asked, "Can we have a good time this weekend? Maybe you can pretend to love me so Shonda could get jealous and run back to me."

She said, "You are stupid. Yes, I am your date for the weekend. Let's have a good time. Now we got to hurry up so that we are not sitting next to the bathroom on the bus."

———————

Deacon Jerry Rhodes rang Shonda's doorbell.

She said, "I am on my way down." She finally opened the door.

He said, "Hey, beautiful. Let me get your bags for you."

"Thanks, Jerry. We must hurry. I want to choose a good seat," Shonda said.
"How many people will be riding this bus?"

"I am not sure. Most of my girls. Oh, and London and his date."

Jerry said, "Mr. Comedian, the man of the year. Shonda, I have no idea what you ever saw in him."

She said, "London is really a sweet guy. I have no idea why he acts like that around you."

"I know why. He knows that you are going to be my wife this time next year," Jerry said.

Shonda laughed hysterically. "Why would you say that? Are we dating exclusively? Because if so, someone forgot to tell me."

"I really do not know what we are doing. All I know is I'm crazy about you, and I believe that this weekend will let us know the direction we are going in."

Shonda wondered what that direction would be as she and Jerry left for E's Place. She clearly wasn't over London.

PACKING THE BUS

Hector brought out one hundred prepared lunches and fifty bags with fresh fruit, vegetables, and ranch dip. There were one hundred assorted sandwiches that included 10 veggie sandwiches. Plus, the cooler had one hundred bottles of water and assorted sodas. The other containers had mixed drinks that included margaritas, Pink Panties, and Sex on the Beach.

He said, "Here you go, Ms. Nikki."

Nikki said, "Perfect, Hector. I love you."

"You see, Ms. Nikki. I listen. Enjoy your trip. Remember who the boss is when Eric is gone," Hector said.

She said, "Hector, you are the boss," Nikki hugged him.

Then the guests began to arrive.

Eric hopped on the bus first. He said, "Baby, where are we sitting?"

Nikki said, "I am hosting some games, so we are sitting behind the driver. Where are the kids?"

"All of them had other things to do, so they will not be coming with us," Eric replied.

Nikki tried to contain her excitement about them being alone without the kids. Shonda and Jerry Rhodes boarded the bus next, followed by Sam, Peace, and Tim.

Nikki said, "Did all you come together?"

Peace said, "No, Sam and I met Tim in the parking lot when we were walking towards the bus."

Nikki joked with her. "I was about to say what freaky deaky stuff y'all got going on."

A man suddenly cleared his throat behind them. He said, "Ladies."

"Pastor Mark Taylor, hey. Where is your beautiful wife?" Nikki asked.

"Here I am," Lisa said as she climbed the steps of the bus.

"And we are here as well," Jackie and Barry said at the same time.

Peace said, "Jackie, you mean to tell me that we beat you here."

"Yes, Peace. It's all Barry's fault," Jackie said.

"What, my fault!" he said.

Another voice broke through the conversation. "Richie is here everyone. Don't love on me all at once. We can now start the bus and ride off in the sunset," he said.

Jackie said, "Hey Richie, Dr. Smith, and you, too, Velma."

They all greeted each other. Jackie tried to be nice to Velma. She said, "You are looking lovely as always."

Velma said, "Thanks, Jackie. You as well."

Eric jumped up and said, "My boy, London. You made it." They bumped fists.

London said, "E, my main man. I am here. You remember my date, Diane."

Someone else suddenly caught London's attention. He said, "Hey Shonda, I am here."

Diane slapped London on the back of his neck and folded her arms across her chest.

Shonda said, "Hello, London. Do not be so rude. Speak to Jerry, please."

London said, "Rude? You did not speak to Diane. Now that's rude. But anyway. . .Hi, Jerry."

Jerry said, "London. Hi, Diane. Nice to see you again." Shonda rolled her eyes at London.

Everyone had finally arrived and were on the bus. Now Nikki could go over the bus rules.

NIKKI STANDS TO SPEAK

Nikki said, "May I please have everyone's attention? First, on behalf of everyone, we would like to thank Sam & Peace Evans for obtaining this bus for us. We were all happy to hear that a bus would be provided for us to get to the ranch."

Everyone on the bus clapped.

Nikki continued speaking. "Secondly, this is a six-hour trip to the ranch. The bus driver has informed me that he will stop for twenty minutes every two hours so that we can stretch our legs. So, if we all can refrain from doing number two, the entire bus will appreciate it."

Applause was heard again.

"Now on to the good stuff. Jackie and I have created some games for the bus ride, and everyone will be participating," Nikki said.

London shouted out. "Is it spin the bottle?"

Everyone laughed.
Nikki said, "No, stupid. It's not spin the bottle."

London placed his hands up in surrender. He said, "Easy, Nikki. it is just a joke." He winked his eye at Shonda.

44

Nikki said, "I am going to explain our first game. In this bag, we have numbers 1-25 twice. Each pair of numbers will sit next to each other. Now to make it juicy. The men will pull from one bag and the women from the other bag."

Nikki opened one of the bags. "Ladies first." Each lady pulled her number.

She said, "Ladies, do not tell anyone what your number is." Nikki grabbed the other bag. "Now men you pull from this one."

After the men picked their numbers, Nikki said, "Who has number one?"

Peace and Tim raised their hands.

Nikki said, "Okay, number one's come sit here."

Then she called the number two. Diane and Eric raised their hands. Nikki said, "The two's take your seat in the last row in the back of the bus. Diane, I got my eye on you. I do not know you like that."
Everyone else was matched up: Shonda with London. Lisa with Dr. Scott. Velma with Sam. Deacon Rhodes with Jackie. Richard with Nikki.

Nikki said, "Since we are all matched up now, here is your questionnaire. Your job is to interview each other. Pry deep into each other lives. Find out who they are and what secrets they are holding. Then you'll have two minutes to discuss them with the bus."

London turned to Shonda and said, "I know a secret about you. I busted that cherry." Only he and Shonda heard what he said. She stood up and started beating on London.

Shonda said, "Nikki, I need a redo. I do not want to be London's partner."

Nikki asked, "Why? The bus wants to know why."

"Because I hate him," Shonda said.

London said, "How can you say that when—"

Shonda placed her hand over his mouth. She said, "I need everyone on this bus to pray for me right now."

The bus broke out into laughter. Then everybody started asking their assigned partners questions.

Tim said, "Peace, what is your deepest secret?"

"I believe all my secrets are out in the open. Everyone knows that I have had trouble conceiving a child. What about you? What is your biggest secret?"

"Peace, this may not be the most appropriate, but I cannot quit thinking about my new client's wife. That is my secret," Tim said.

Peace screamed. "You know that I can't repeat that secret out loud if you want to keep your job with my husband."

Tim said, "I know, but what should we do about it?"
Peace said, "Absolutely nothing. I am a married woman whose husband has decided to run for mayor. I cannot afford for any of my secrets, even the one I cannot remember to come out. You already know his opponents will be searching high and low to disgrace him any way they can. Like the two women that he has cheated on me with, plus children he has fathered. Whatever they can find."

Tim said, "You are correct. Let's talk about the time I cheated on my chemistry paper while I was at Yale because I was out partying and not studying."

They both laughed.

Nikki stood up and said, "Okay, two minutes are up. Who wants to go first?"

Peace raised her hand. She said, "Tim once cheated on a test while he was a student at Yale."

Tim said, "Peace is scared that Sam may become the next mayor of Sterling."

Nikki said, "London, you are next."

"Okay, everyone. Shonda confessed that she still liked me," he said.

Shonda punched London and said, "He is such a liar. I hate him. London confessed that he once paid $1.000.00 on a dress for a woman."

London said, "Shonda! That was our little secret."

Nikki said, "Okay, everyone. Who is next?"

The game of confession went on for the next hour until they finally made it to the first rest stop. Hank, the bus driver, yelled out. "Listen up, we have four more hours to go and two more twenty-minute stops. Please everyone get off the bus, stretch your legs, and kindly do number two if you have to. The time is now, but the quicker you return, the sooner we can leave. I will pull off without you."

As everyone exited the bus, Jerry grabbed Shonda's hand. He said, "I see why London is so crazy about you. You are absolutely breathtaking."

Shonda said, "Thank you, Deacon. You are not so bad yourself, Mr. Sexy."

Jerry asked, "What is the next game that we will be playing?"

Shonda said, "You know, I have no idea. But with these people, it is no telling."

AFTER THE REST STOP

"London's nose is wide open around Shonda. He is not over her," Mark said.

"How can you tell?" Lisa asked.

He replied, "It is obvious by the way he acts like a little kid around her."

She said, "Shonda needs a real man, not a little boy. Jerry is who I am rooting for."

"It is not up to us who she lays with," Mark said.

"The Devil is a lie! It is up to us to lead them into the pearly gates of heaven," Lisa replied.

Mark said, "And you do not think that London is good for her. Why?"

"I just do not like him," she said. "I would like to see Shonda and Jerry become that couple that we hang out with. I really do not see that with anyone else in our circle of friends."

Mark said, "I can see what you are saying, Lisa. But it must be Shonda's decision if she will begin to date Jerry seriously, not yours. Okay? As the first lady of our church, you must conduct yourself as a person that minds her own business and not pass judgment on others. You do know that eventually most of the ladies in the church will begin coming to you with their situations. You can't be that "SNOOTY" little bitch you once were when we were married before. Do you understand me?"

Lisa said quietly, "Yes, Mark."

Jackie and Nikki took the lead as everyone walked back in pairs like a large wedding party to the coach bus. Jackie mused over the responses to the first game they had played. She had to admit. Nikki was quite the event planner.

Jackie said, "Nikki, that game was great. What is the next game that we are playing once everyone returns to the bus?"

Nikki said, "Charades, then name that tune. With charades, I will have everyone's name in the bag. Each person will then pull a name, mimic that person with three words, and then pose." They both laughed.

Laughter filled the bus as everybody went back to their seats. Hank asked, "Is everyone all aboard?"

Nikki said, "Attention, we are about to take off. Look around and see if everyone is present."

Eric replied, "No. London had to run back in for his phone."

Someone said, "Leave him." Everyone on the bus burst into laughter.

Shonda said, "Jerry! That's not nice."

"He can be a jerk sometimes," he replied.

She said, "That may be true. However, leaving him in the middle of no man's land is not the solution."

Jerry asked, "Tell me the truth. Do you still like him?"

Shonda said, "Like I said before, London came in my life during a time that I was at my lowest. He made me feel special and beautiful. I will always appreciate him for that. I will always care about him, but I do not like him in that way. So, do not get it confused."

"I am sorry for sounding like a love-struck, jealous teenager," he said.

Meanwhile, Richard noticed that Velma seemed tense. He thought the coach ride would be a perfect opportunity to snuggle and reconnect.

He said, "How are you feeling, sweetheart?"

"I am great. I just hate that any place we go as a group, it must be with that damn Jackie. She always wants all of the attention even when it is not about her," Velma said.

Richard said, "She is in my inner circle. If I may be frank with you, she *is* the circle. Now if you get out more and meet other people on our level or hang out with some of the other doctors' wives, I will be more than happy to join you. However, do not be so surprised if it seems like they are trying to join this circle here."

Velma said, "What surprises me the most is you always take up for her."

Richard said, "No, not at all, but I know what I am talking about. So, we can leave this alone before we have a nasty weekend over nothing. Just admit that you do not like my friend, Jackie."

Velma said, "Yes, Richard, you are correct on both. We are going to leave this alone, and I do not like that bitch, Jackie."

As Velma continued to give Richard the side eye, Peace tries hard to put her game face on, so she doesn't reveal Tim's true secret to Sam.

Sam beamed with pride about his idea working out well so far. He said, "Aren't you glad that we got this bus?"

Peace said, "Yes, I am. That first game was quite interesting. I learned a lot about Tim."

Sam said, "That is good because he is going to be around for a while. He's a great choice for a campaign manager."

Peace nodded in agreement. She didn't know about Tim as Sam's choice for his campaign manager. He's too damn fine to be around her. Sam may have another scandal to worry about.

As Sam and Peace continued their conversation, Jackie joked around with Barry.

Jackie said, "As you can see, this group is crazy."

He said, "I can see that. I'm also looking at the ringleader."

"Barry! Why did you say that? I'm not the only crazy one on this bus," she said.

He said, "Absolutely! Most of the women on this bus are a nut. I should have gone into psychiatry. I could have made a fortune off you and your friends alone."

Jackie's mouth opened wide in response, but then she laughed. Barry just dropped some truth about her and the crew.

Nikki watched Jackie flirt with Barry as she admired her handiwork. She said, "Eric, all the food and drinks are a hit. Did you enjoy the first game?"

He said, "I really did. I learned a lot about Velma."

"Great. I hope you enjoy the next two games. They will lead up to you endorsing Sam as our next mayor," she said.

Before Eric could respond, Nikki stood up again to address everyone. She said, "Okay, everyone one. Please eat and drink up. Let's get ready for our next game. It's Charades. You will pick a name from the bag. You must say three words that the person says often and pose like them. We will have one minute to guess who it is. Who is first to pick? "

Mark raised his hand and said, "Let me get this torture out the way. I'll go first." Then he says in a deep voice, "Good evening, ladies."

People started shouting out names.

"Eric!"
"Sam!"
"Henry!"
"Lisa!"

Nikki said, "The minute is up. Who is it?"

Mark responded, "It's Dr. Barry Scott."

Jackie yelled out. "You didn't sound sexy enough."

Mark said, "Well, excuse me, Jackie. I thought I sounded even better than Dr. Scott."

Lisa chimed in. "That's right, baby. You sounded much sexier than him."

"Thank you, my gorgeous wife, Madam Lisa." Mark and Lisa kissed each other.

"Whatever, you horny newlyweds," Nikki said. "Dr. Scott, since he picked your name, you're up next."

"Thanks, I'm ready," Barry said as he drew a name from the bag. "Ok. I'm in the house."

Five people screamed out. "London!"
Barry said, "Yes, he was easy."

Diane muttered, "Yeah, too easy with the ladies. With his charismatic ass."

Eric came to his boy's defense. said, "Don't hate the player. Hate the game." Nikki slapped him on the back of his head. "What? I'm just saying."

London loved the attention. He said, "People listen. I must announce myself, so the ladies would know that I'm here. Right, Shonda?"

Shonda frowned as she yelled. "London! Leave me alone. How should I know?"

London said, "Oh, Shonda, you *want* to know when I'm in the house."

"London!" Shonda rubbed her temples in aggravation.

"Nikki, is it my turn?" he asked.

"Come on up here and quit aggravating my friend," she said.

"Nikki, I can't help that she likes me," London said.

The entire bus laughed—everyone but Jerry. He said, "Shonda, just say the word! Say the word! I will go up there and beat the hell out of your silly ass friend. I have no idea how a woman of your caliber dated a FOOL like him."

London smirked as he held up his hands. He said, "You didn't say nothing but a word, my man."

Shonda said, "Jerry, calm down. He's just trying to aggravate me and you. We will not allow him to ruin our weekend before it begins. After all, I'm here with you."

Jerry said, "You are correct. I have the true prize, which is you." He kissed her long and passionately until London cleared his throat. Diane punched him on his arm and turned her back to him.

For the next couple of hours, people continued to play games, eat, nap, and drink.

TIM & SAM SPEAK TO EVERYONE

With thirty minutes to spare before their arrival to the ranch, Tim stood up with the microphone in his hand.

He said, "May I please have everyone's attention? For those that don't know me, I am Tim Ross, Mr. Sam Evans' campaign manager. I just want you to know that this was not a campaign gesture. Your friends, Sam and Peace, thought of this all on their own. They truly knew that most people were tired."

Everyone stood up and clapped.

Tim said, "Now just so you know, Sam. I will steal this idea for my next client."

Everyone laughed.

Sam stood up. He said, "Thank you all very much for the standing ovation. I truly appreciate it, but it's not necessary. Everyone on this bus was an invited guest of me or my wife. On Wednesday, we were still so tired that we didn't feel like driving six hours to the ranch ourselves. We didn't want to postpone it until next weekend because most of us had already rearranged our schedules, and this has been our tradition for how long, Jackie? "

She said, "Over twenty-five years, Sam."

Sam said, "We can't break that. We have so much to be thankful for."

He extended his arm and held his hand out to each person in the crowd. "Jackie's new matchmaking company. Eric & Nikki's successful restaurant. Reverend Mark Taylor & Lisa's surprise wedding. And yes, me running for mayor and trying to fill my dad's shoes."

Everyone applauded and cheered. Barry patted Jackie on the back, while the two couples embraced each other as Sam continued.

He said, "Let me tell you all something. I'm scared to death. Sure, I know how to run a multimillion-dollar business. But, running a city—" Sam bent his head down and rubbed the bridge of his nose. The weight of the campaign settled on his shoulders.

He said, "Having all of my indiscretions exposed to the entire city, hoping and praying that my wife continues to stand by my side once all of it is brought up again."

Sam turned toward his wife, Peace. Her eyes, sympathetic and compassionate, held his. Her eyes were on him, but her mind still entertained the attraction between her and Tim.
Sam said, "Peace, I love you just as much now as I did on the day that I married you. I will spend the rest of my life making up to you the pain that I have caused. Now, if you feel this is going to be too much, just say so and I won't run. I won't try to talk you into it at all. It's up to you, my dear. Will you give me the green light to run for mayor of our beautiful town, Sterny?"

Peace greeted her husband with a kiss. She said, "Yes, Sam. I am willing to be your first lady if I got my girls' support because I'm going to need it. What do you say, girls?"

Jackie said, "Yes."

Shonda said, "Absolutely."

Lisa said, "You don't even have to ask."

Nikki remained quiet.

Peace said, "Aw, Nikki. Will you be by my side?"

"I knew you loved me," Nikki said.

Peace said, "You have grown on me."

"Hell, yes. Peace, I'm here," Nikki said.

Peace then said, "And you, too, Velma. Any wife of Richard is a friend of ours."

Velma said, "Thank you so much, Peace. I will truly be honored to assist you."

"Thank you, ladies," Peace said.

London blurted out. "Excuse me, Peace. What about my girl?"

Peace was a little taken aback. She said, "I'm sorry. Have I met her yet?"

Diane said, "I'm sorry for my date's rudeness. I don't even live here half of the time. However, when I'm home, I'll contact the campaign office to see how I may be of some assistance when I'm available, if that's okay."

Tim stood up and replied, "That would be great, Diane. We will need all the help we can get whenever you are available. Thank you, everyone. We now have a race."

Hank announced, "Ladies and gentlemen, we should arrive at the Evans Ranch in about five minutes, and I'll see you on Sunday afternoon at 1:00p.m. for your return trip to Sterny. It has been a pleasure being your driver today."

THE ARRIVAL AT THE RANCH

Hank said, "Please exit the bus slowly and grab hold to the rails as you step down, considering some of you have consumed several cocktail beverages. Your luggage can be retrieved at the back of the bus."

As everybody gathered to the back of the bus, they turned their heads when London yelled out.

He said, "Hey Stanley, my main man, and the lovely Tara Welch."

Stanley said, "We made it."

London said, "Well, Diane and I are glad to see you."

Sam walked up to the men. He said, "Hey, Stanley. How long have you all been here?"

He said, "We got here about an hour ago. Maggie let us in, so I chose my usual room that I usually get."

Sam said, "Man, Stanley. You know Jackie is going to go off."

Stanley said, "Not really. You and I both know that she doesn't like being embarrassed in front of people she really doesn't know. Here comes your beautiful wife."

"Hi, Peace. How are you feeling today?" he said.

Peace said, "I'm great, Stanley. Thanks for asking. I'm sorry. How are you. . . um. . .um?"

"Tara." She shook Peace's extended hand. "My name is Tara Welch," she said.

Peace said, "Excuse me. I know that I met you at my party, but there were so many new people this year that I couldn't remember everyone's name."

"That's not a problem, Peace. Thank you for inviting us," Tara said.

Peace directed her attention to Stanley. She said "So, why didn't you RSVP?"

Stanley said, "It seems as if I am the only one that plays by the rules. Why should I miss my frat's wife's event because my ex-wife may be uncomfortable with my beautiful, new young woman?"

"Stanley!" Peace said sharply.
Stanley began to explain. He said, "I am through playing by Jackie's rules. She cheated on me, and I know that all of you knew about it. You guys probably helped her to cover it up. Nevertheless, I'm not blaming anyone for our breakup—"

Peace said, "We were all just as shocked as you were about Jackie's infidelity. You know what I have gone through in my life. You should know that I don't uphold any wrong. I don't care who it is."

Stanley said, "Well, I'm over it now, and we are moving on. The only thing that we didn't divide in the divorce is our friends. We all went to college together and for the last twenty-five years or more, we have shared both great times and sad times. Plus, I am still a good friend as well,"

Peace gave him a quick hug. She said, "Stanley, sweetie, you are still our friend. Come on in and enjoy your weekend."

He said, "Thank you, Peace. I love you, girl. What time is dinner tonight?"

"Late evening, probably around 6:30-7p.m. We are really exhausted." Peace said her goodbyes to Stanley and Tara. As she walked toward the cabin's entrance, she heard him telling Tara to let him show her around the ranch.

During this time, everybody had obtained their cabin keys and room assignments from the host. As Jackie got to the front desk, she found out that her husband had already checked in, and he had both sets of keys.

Jackie said to the host, "Stanley and I are no longer together. Can I have another suite?"

The host said, "I'm so sorry, Ms. Lewis. I have two rooms available: one with a standard king-size bed or one with two full-size beds. We are all out of suites."

Jackie clenched her teeth. "I am going to hurt him!" she said.

Barry said, "What's wrong, babe? Tell me what's wrong."

She said, "That ex-husband of mine stole our romantic fireplace suite for him and his little bimbo."

"Sweetheart, it doesn't matter which room we are in. We can sleep outside or in a tent. As long as I'm with you, that's all I care about," Barry said. Then the two of them kissed passionately.

Now everybody had gone to their rooms and settled in; then the whispers began.

BEHIND CLOSED DOORS

Mark and Lisa began unpacking their luggage. They could hear Shonda and Jerry doing the same thing in the adjoining room of their cabin. Mark hoped that Deacon was being a gentleman, while Lisa thought about her previous conversation with Mark and the events that happened on the bus.

She said, "This is going to be an interesting weekend."

Mark said, "I agree as I see Jackie's and Shonda's situations unfold. I am so glad that we never brought anyone else in our circle. It's very hard on us. They are our friends, and we love them both,"

Lisa stopped what she was doing. She said firmly, "We don't like London."

He replied, "We liked London last year."

"No, we accepted London last year because that was the first man that Shonda ever brought around us. But Jerry is the guy for her. He's a Godly man, a family man, a hardworking, loyal, and honest man. Just what Shonda needs. Not some 40-year-old man still acting like a frat boy all of the time," Lisa said.

Mark said, "Please mind your own damn business when it comes to Shonda and her love life. We must respect her choice. Do you understand me?"

Lisa said softly, "Yes, Mark."

_____

"Eric, do you think Peace meant what she said about feeling as if I'm a friend of hers?" Nikki asked.

He replied, "Absolutely. She knows you have been just as much of a friend as the other ladies in the group. Come on, mama. Bring that big old ass over here and give me a quickie before dinner."

"Boy that's all you ever think about."

"Not true, Nikki. Not anymore," he said.

"The bulge in your pants says otherwise," Nikki said with a laugh.
"Now I also have to think about the restaurant, payroll, inventory, and my kids. Having a beautiful woman to help me release some tension makes it worthwhile," Eric said. "Now bring your fine ass over here."

"Here I come, boy. You so nasty," Nikki said.

"You know that's the way you like it," Eric said before he showed her how nasty he really could be.

_____

Meanwhile, Richard and Velma rested on the sofa inside their room.

Richard said, "I told you the girls were going to come around and accept you."

"Have they truly accepted me, or are they looking for supporters to help with Sam's campaign?" Velma asked.

"My love, you are looking at this all wrong. The fact that she said you were in her clique proves you are in" Richard said.

Velma said, "I believe she said, and I quote, 'And you, too, Velma. Any wife of Richard is a friend of ours.'"

Richard said, "Baby, you better get in where you can fit in."

"Why, Richard? Because you think this group is the end all be all?" Velma let out a wicked laugh. "Oh, I can't wait to see how the rest of this weekend goes with Jackie, her husband, and her boyfriend situation."

He said, "Velma, that is so evil."

"That bitch shouldn't think that it's ok to treat her husband like that," Velma said.

Richard said, "What the hell are you talking about? They are divorced. Jackie and Stanley still share friends in a mature way. Now I need you to try and get better acquainted with my friends and pretend like you care about someone other than yourself."

Velma couldn't believe Richard right now. She said, "I can be friends with some of them, but that skank, Jackie—never. I don't know who you think you are fooling, but you two were more than just friends. 'We've been friends since we were twelve-years-old, my ass.'"

———————

Jerry asked, "Why did you order a room with two beds?"

Shonda said, "I'm not exactly sure what we are doing. Are we a couple? Is this just another date? I don't know where we stand. We've never discussed it."

Jerry said, "Let's talk now. Will you marry me?"

"What! Jerry Rhodes, quit playing. Are you serious?" Shonda said.

"Yes, Shonda. Marry me, please. You won't regret it." He grabbed her face and kissed her.

She said, "This is ludicrous. Is this because of London?"

Jerry said, "No, it is not. It's truly because I am in love with you and only you."

Shonda said, "I'm not saying no, but please let's get to know each other a lot better first."

"I'll be patient and wait. But I will propose to you again real soon," Jerry said.

All Shonda could think about was making love to London. She hoped that London was not doing to Diane what he did to her when they had sex.

———————

In London and Diane's room, Shonda was the main topic of their conversation.

Diane said, "London, I am not here this weekend to look like a fool with you. Everyone here, including myself, realizes that you are clearly not over Shonda. If you love her and want to be with her, then confess your love to her and quit acting stupid around her."

London said, "You are so right. She drives me crazy, and yes, I am still in love with her. I tried to tell her how I felt, but now she has this egghead, funny-looking ass deacon chasing up behind her. Plus, it doesn't help that her good friend, First Lady Lisa, wants her with him."

Diane said, "Trust me. You are not going to win her over acting silly. It's funny, but she can't take you seriously. If you want, I'll help you win her over this weekend. However, you must do as I say and follow my lead. Do we have a deal?"

"Diane, we have a deal." London and Diane shook hands.

———————————

Peace said, "This may turn out to be our craziest weekend getaway yet."

Sam said, "My love, I believe you may be correct. I know you well. What do you have in mind?"

Peace laughed. "Baby, you do know me. This is what I was thinking. Instead of the staff setting us up like one long banquet table tonight, I'm going to have him set everyone up at private Cabernet tables with mini vases of a single red rose and a baby's breath flower. It will work out fine since everyone here is a couple and no children are here."

Sam said, "You are forgetting about Tim and your sister, Gina. They are here alone, and they are not a couple."

Peace said, "No, they are not, but they will just have to sit together tonight. Because I'm afraid we may have a fistfight this weekend."

Sam said, "Between London and Jerry or Jackie and Stanley?"

Peace said, "You are hilarious. Let me call the banquet room now."

———————

Tara was enjoying Stanley's tour of the ranch. She said, "This ranch is beautiful. What did Peace's other ranch look like?"

Stanley said, "The other ranch was just as nice, but less amenities. This one has the stable for her new horses that she got for her birthday last year and the inground pool house, game room, and a banquet room that I understand they are renting out every weekend for events."

Tara said, "Did you and Jackie invest in anything like this?"

"We're not into real estate like that. Sam has always been into buying and selling homes, and I'm his investment attorney," Stanley said.

"Sometimes I feel like you are just using me to make her jealous. Are you? What are your plans for us?" she asked.

"Well, I'm going to make love to you so damn good that you are going to be screaming my name so loud. I'm going to have every woman on this ranch wanting a piece of me," he replied.

She laughed and said, "Who said I am going to give you some? I'm not interested in sleeping with a man that is still in love with his wife and won't even admit it. You do realize I have feelings, too."

He said, Yes, I know that you have feelings, and yes, I will always love Jackie because she's the mother of my kids and my business partner. I'm over her. You are all I want and need."

Stanley kissed her on the neck. "You are my lady now. I hope you know how much you really mean to me."

Tara said, "I know how I feel when we are home, but not when we are here. When you come here, you become someone else."

Stanley said, "I'm so sorry if I make you feel like that. Come here, and let me show you how much I truly care."

———————————

Peace said, "I just finished up with all the arrangements for tonight."

Sam said, "Well, my love, what time is dinner?"

"It is 6:00p.m. for appetizers and cocktails, and 7:00p.m. for dinner time. I just sent out a group text. Don't forget that our first dinner is formal," Peace said.

He said, "Do I have to wear a tux for tonight?"

She said, "No, Sammy Bear, you can wear a suit with a tie, please."

Sam said, "Okay, then. You better start getting ready."

Peace said, "We have almost three hours before we need to be there."

Sam said, "True, but that's how long it takes you to get ready."

———————————

Tim looked at his cell phone. Peace just texted him. Maybe she was about to sneak over to his room. What was he thinking? Why out of all the women in the world he had to have a crush on this one? Tim couldn't figure out what it was about Peace that he couldn't get over. He remembered the first time he ever met her. He felt like she deserved better, and that better was him. Tim whispered to himself as he stared into the bathroom mirror. "Let me shake this shit off."

He was making a bunch of money off this gig and couldn't afford to mess it up. If Tim could help Sam win this election for mayor, it would solidify him a position in the mayor's office. He had to shake this shit off.

Tim threw some cold water on his face and began to get ready for the formal dinner.

ENTERING THE BANQUET

Sam said, "Honey, we have about thirty minutes before we must leave. Come in here before you slide your dress on and talk to me real quick."

Peace said, "Look, don't make me blush. Besides, thirty minutes have never been enough time for you. So, I'm going to take a rain check for later on tonight. I really don't want to be late because of the changes in the seating arrangements. Plus, I must introduce Tim and my sister, Gina. I don't want them to think I'm trying to make them a couple. "

Sam said, "But it's not my fault that I may have a print showing. This hard won't go down by itself without some type of help."

"Sam! Please behave, and let's get ready to go to dinner," Peace said.

As everybody scrambled around to prepare for dinner, they eventually made their way to the banquet room.

Peace and Sam were the first to arrive. She asked the banquet manager to assist her with seating each couple.

Peace joined Sam by the door as they greeted their first guests, Lisa and Mark.

Lisa said, "Oh my God! This is such a beautiful room."

Peace said, "Yes, it is. I have my wonderful husband to thank for all of this. Here are your gift bags."

Shonda and Jerry entered at the same time as London and Diane.
London said, "Good evening, Sam and Peace. What a lovely establishment you have here. Maybe next year, we'll be hosting a wedding here."

Peace said, "I didn't realize you and Diane were so serious."

Diane rubbed her finger across London's face and said, "A lot has happened with London and me. Who knows? Love is truly in the air."

Peace said, "If you say so." She handed them their gift bags. "You guys are seated at table fifteen."

Shonda and Jerry stood in front of Peace and Sam. Peace said to Jerry, "How do you like the ranch?"

"It is absolutely breathtaking. I love it. This is a picture-perfect venue," Jerry said.

Peace said, "Perhaps for a wedding? London just told me that we may be hosting one here next year."

She handed the gift bags to Shonda and said, "You are assigned to table number twenty-one."

Shonda knew that London couldn't be thinking about marrying Diane after the way he made love to her.

Jerry said, "Let's stop by Rev. Taylor's table and speak."

She said, "Sure, let's go. See you later, Peace."

Stanley, Tara, and Timothy walked in together.

Sam said, "Stanley, my main man. Tara, you look stunning."

Peace said, "I love that dress."

Tara said, "Thank you. That means a lot to me coming from you. And thank you as well, Sam."

Stanley said, "Sam, you are the man. I love this venue. Peace, I love the romantic illusion you have chosen for tonight. The candles are a nice touch."

"Well, I love it, too. But I'm feeling a little left out of the love category here," Tim said.

Peace kissed Tim on the cheek. She said, "It's not a date, but you'll be sitting at the table with my sister, Gina."

Stanley shouted out, "It's a blind date!"

"Stanley!" Peace said.

Stanley said, "Look, my man. At least her sister is fine. A little crazy, but in a cute and sexy way."

Peace said, "Stanley, you and Tara are at table nine. Here are your gift bags."

He said, "Thanks Peace. You're setting my man up. Let's go mingle for a minute, Tara."

Peace turned to Tim and said, "I'm sorry that we didn't ask your permission first. You two are the only single people here, and we didn't want you to stay in your rooms this evening. Will you forgive us, please?"

Tim said, "Sam, your wife is a mess."

Sam said, "Man, Tim, who you telling. But look who's walking up." Sam turned to Peace's sister. "Gina, how are you, my love?"

Gina said, "When did we start setting up the tables like this for the banquet dinner party?"

Sam said, "Since Peace and I felt like we might have a fight on our hands if we didn't."

Gina said, "What? Who's trying to start something, Sam?"

Peace said, "I'll explain later. I promise you. However, this is Tim, our campaign manager. You two will be sitting together for dinner, if that's ok with the both of you?"

Gina said, "Well, you guys didn't leave us much of a choice, did you? And since we don't want to miss the fight, if it's going to be one, we'll stay."

Tim said, "Hello Gina. You are looking great this evening."

"Thank you, Tim. You aren't looking so bad yourself. Shall we proceed to our seats?" she asked.

He replied, "That sounds like a great idea. What's our table number, Peace?"

Peace gave them their gift bags. She said, "Table four, and thank you guys so much."

Tim held his elbow out for Gina to grab his arm and away they went. Everybody burst out laughing.

Sam greeted Dr. Richard Smith and his beautiful wife, Velma. "Welcome to our fine establishment."

Velma said, "This place is gorgeous."

"Well, not as gorgeous as you, Velma," Sam replied.

Velma thanked him and said to Peace, "How are you? I love this place."

Peace said, "I'm fine. You are at table twenty-two." She handed them their gift bags and said, "Enjoy your evening."

Barry & Jackie walked quickly behind them. Jackie said, "Hey, hey, we are here. Best friend, you are looking spectacular."

Peace said, "Thank you. Hi, Dr. Scott. How are you tonight?"

Barry replied, "Well, Mr. and Mrs. Evans, I'm doing fine. But judging by the way this place, it looks like you all are doing much better."

Sam said, "So, Dr. Scott, is it safe to say that we have the doctor's approval?"

Barry laughed and said, "Absolutely. Sam, this place is nice."

Peace said, "Thank you, Dr. Scott. That means a whole lot coming from you." Peace handed them their gift bags. "Jackie, you guys are at table two next to Sam and me."

"Thanks, honey. Did Nikki and Eric arrive yet?" Jackie asked.

Peace said, "Speak of the devil. Look who's walking in."

Nikki said, "Hey girls!"

Jackie and Peace both replied simultaneously. "Hello Nikki."

"Y'all talking about all of this fineness again?" Nikki said.

Peace said, "Heavens no, Nikki."

Eric said, "Peace, you are truly looking lovely tonight."

"What about me, man? How do I look?"

"You are my dog. We are frat brothers for life. I look good, so you look better," Eric said.

Sam got serious for a minute. He said, "I'm so grateful to God for you. Thanks for being in my corner."

Eric said, "Sam, you got it."

Peace gave them their gift bags and said, "I believe you and Nikki are at table three."

Nikki said, "Peace, we gonna have a ball up in here tonight." She said to Jackie, "What table are you at?"

Jackie said "Two."

Nikki said, "Ok, girl. Come on, let's go to our table. See you guys in a minute."

Jackie said, "Nikki, let's mingle a little bit first."
Barry nudged Eric on the elbow and said. "You know we are in trouble tonight."

Eric said, "I got a feeling that we all are in trouble the whole weekend."

DINNER TIME

Sam and Peace stood at their table. He picked up his knife and tapped it against his champagne glass. Everybody finished mingling and were now seated. Sam cleared his throat to speak. "First and foremost, I would like to give honor to God, who is the head of the entire Evans family."

"Amen," Pastor Mark said.

He smiled at him and continued. "Next, my wife and I would like to thank you again for taking the time to share this weekend with us. It is an honor for us to have each and every last one of you here. We have an exceptional weekend planned for everyone."

Peace said, "Now please keep in mind that everything is optional. If you and your significant other would prefer to stay indoors, that's fine. Room service is extension #22. Tie the red scarf on the doorknob, and everyone will know not to interrupt. People, please respect the red scarf."

Sam said, "Before dinner is served, I must have my good friend, my brother, and my spiritual advisor, Reverend Mark Taylor to come up and bless the food. Come on up, Pastor."

Everyone stood and applauded.

Mark said, "May I have every head in this room bowed for prayer?"

All heads were bowed except for one. With one eye opened, London turned to stare at Shonda. Diane gripped his neck and forced it down as she whispered in his ear to remember the plan.

Mark prayed, "Now God, we come to you with a humble spirit. We ask that You bless the food and the hands that prepared it. We ask, God, that this food is providing nothing but nourishment to our bodies and that You cover everyone throughout this resort. God, keep us safe and in sound mind and in one piece. In Jesus' name. Amen!"

The servers came out with the food in Brazilian style. They carried pork, chicken, steak, and shrimp on a stick. The servers placed salads, potatoes, and fresh roasted vegetables on the tables. After two hours of food and drinks, it was time to turn up the party. Everybody was so full, but they knew they needed to dance some of the calories off.

London started it off as he hit the dance floor and yelled out to Diane. "Come on, let's cut a rug."

Diane said, "Don't get me up here and embarrass me."

London said, "What you talking 'bout, Diane?"

"London. Behave," Diane warned playfully.

"Bring all that sexiness here," he said. They were soon joined on the dance floor by Eric and Nikki, Jackie and Barry, then a few others. Lisa, Mark, Shonda, and Jerry remained seated.

Lisa said, "Let's go on the dance floor."

Mark said, "Don't start. You are a first lady."

"So, does this mean we can't have fun at our friends' party?" Lisa asked.

"Come on, but no twerking out there. Do you hear me?" Mark said.

Jackie noticed Lisa and Mark dancing. She said, "Hey, Mark, you still got it."

Mark smiled and said, "I hope so, Jackie."

Meanwhile, Jerry wondered why Shonda hadn't moved yet. He said, "Everyone is on the dance floor but us. Now why is that?"

Shonda said, "Well, Jerry. I'm not a good dancer."

"Neither is your ex, but he's out there making a fool out of himself and having fun," he said.

"I just didn't want to embarrass you," she said nervously.

He said, "There is absolutely nothing you can do to embarrass me. You are too damn fine for that. "

"You are too kind, Jerry. Are you trying to make me fall in love with you this weekend?"

"Not only this weekend, Shonda, but for the rest of your life."

Shonda didn't understand where all of this talk of love and marriage was coming from with Jerry. Did he really love her, or was he just competing with London?

Jerry was a deacon, a respectable man in Sterny. Any woman would have wanted to be married to him, but not every woman had lost her virginity to the best lover in the world. London had her wide open. Well, she wished he did tonight.

She said, "Wow! I wasn't ready for that, Jerry."

"Why, Shonda? We've been going out for over a year. Lots of people our age are married and expecting a child by now."

She said, "I can see myself married, yes, Children, no."

Jerry said, "I feel you would make a great wife and an even better mom."

Shonda said, "Oh, Jerry." He always said the sweetest things. They finally made it to the dance floor.

Sam yelled out, "Soul Train line, everyone. Where are my dogs at?"

Stanley stood up and barked as he headed towards the dance floor.

Eric immediately followed, then Tim and Mark as well as a few others. After all, these were some of his frat brothers.

Jackie, Peace, Gina, and Lisa stood in a circle and chanted a song out pertaining to their sorority. After twenty minutes of Greek dancing, everyone was on the dance floor having a great time.

Two hours later, several couples had gone back to their rooms. The girls were all standing in the hallway, laughing and talking.

Jackie said, "Now, Peace. I hope we aren't having an 8a.m. wake-up call for breakfast?"

Peace said, "No. everyone is on their own until about 1p.m."

Nikki asked, "What's happening at 1p.m.?"

"We are going horseback riding and ATVing in the mountains. They are bringing up more horses and four more wheelers in the morning," Peace said.

Shonda said, "I'm so excited!"

Nikki said, "Why are you excited? Are you going to give the good old deacon some tonight?"

"That's none of your business. A true lady doesn't kiss and tell," Shonda replied.

"That's right, Nikki because if Tim kiss me just right tonight, I just might," Gina said.

Peace said, "Gina!"

"You got Sam. I want somebody, too," Gina said.

Peace said, "But, not on the first night."

"Why not?" Nikki asked boldly.

Everyone yells, "Nikki!'

"What! A little sex isn't going to hurt anyone," Nikki said. Everyone laughed as they went to their rooms.

ABOUT LAST NIGHT

Peace and Sam held each other closely. He kissed the side of her neck and her shoulder before moving toward her soft lips.

Peace said, "Mr. Evans, you truly know how to throw a great party."

"Well, Mrs. Evans, you are not too bad yourself. Now please tell me that you aren't too tired to make love to me tonight," he said.

"How many times have I ever told you that I was too tired?" she asked.

"Never, Mrs. Evans. I love you so much. I'm the luckiest man on earth," Sam said.

"Well, why don't you show me?" She led him to their bed.

————————————

Jackie said, "Barry, did you enjoy yourself?"

Barry said, "I truly enjoyed this evening. It's only one thing that could make it better."

"What's that Dr, Scott?" Jackie asked.

Barry undressed and laid on top of the bed. "Come a little closer, and I'll show you." They enjoyed making passionate love the remainder of the night.

———————————

Gina and Tim talked for a little while longer outside her room door.

"I must admit. At first, I was very upset to find out I had a secret blind date," Tim said.

"But what about now?" Gina asked.

Tim answered. "You have turned out to be one of the best dates of my adult life. You were great as a partner today."

"Why, thank you. You were not too bad yourself," Gina said.

Tim gently kissed Gina on her cheek. "Well, I'll see you tomorrow."

Gina replied, "Absolutely."

———————————

Shonda and Jerry talked to each other as they rested on top of their beds.

He said, "I had a ball tonight."

"I had too much fun," she said.

Jerry kept asking the same question. "Where do we go from here?"

Shonda said, "I'm not sure."

He said, "I know which direction I would love to see our relationship go."

Shonda remained silent. Her mind kept racing as she thought about what London and Diane were doing right now. She really was confused about what to do. Shonda hoped that Jerry would not pop the question again.

Jerry said, "Will you marry me?"

"Jerry!" Shonda said.

"I'm serious, and if you say yes, when we get back home you can pick out whatever ring you want. I have about $12,000 set aside just for your ring," he said.

"Oh my God, Jerry. I don't know. I'm scared," she said.

"Shonda, come here." Jerry and Shonda embraced each other, and then they made love.

London and Diane discussed how their plan worked tonight. She noticed that Shonda kept watching him while they were dancing.

She said, "You know if you were not in love with Shonda, we could have a great relationship."

"Was it that obvious tonight?" London asked.

Diane reassured him. "No, on the contrary, you didn't act desperate tonight. That's the only way you are going to win her and her little group over. I told you that after this weekend she'll come running back to you."

He said, "Diane, I'm trusting you. I'll be on the couch. If you feel like giving me a little bit, just call and I'll come running."

A pillow hit London hard in the face. "I guess that's a no," he said.

———————————

Tara and Stanley enjoyed a nightcap in their room. Tara smiled as she reflected on their evening together. She said, "You have truly surprised me these last couple of weeks. Once you loosen up, you are great to be around."

He said, "This is the real me. I'm here around my true friends. When we first met, I was broken, angry, and bitter. I was mad as hell. The life that I thought I had was nothing but a façade. I was embarrassed and thought that everyone knew that my wife was cheating on me."

Tara said, "Oh, Stanley, I'm sorry."

"Why are you sorry? Jackie will never control my life again. I truly loved my wife. I had the same opportunities to cheat on her. Women were always throwing themselves on me, but I assumed we had something special. We were the couple that everyone wanted to be like, so I thought. It was all fake as hell. I promise you. She will regret ever cheating on me," Stanley said.

"It doesn't sound like you are over her," Tara said.

He replied, "To be honest, I am over her. I just want her to feel the pain that she caused our family."

The Tangled Web We Weave

Tara said, "The Bible states, 'Vengeance is mine,' Stanley."

"I know, Tara, but I'm just going to hurry God up just a little bit."

THE MORNING AFTER

Jackie awakened at 5:00a.m. as usual. Last night with Barry was wonderful, she thought. She's not sure if it was great because she hadn't had any in a long while or he was just that good. Well, Jackie guessed there's only way to find out. She kissed Barry on his back and rolled her tongue down his little Barry. He woke up with excitement and made love to Jackie like he had never made love to a woman before.

After round two, Jackie woke up at 8:35a.m. with the biggest smile. Barry was the BOMB. What a wonderful lover. She could definitely get used to that. Damn, Jackie would have loved one more shot, but she would have to take care of that later on tonight. She slid out of the bed and took a quick shower. Jackie got dressed and ran to the workout room.

As Jackie finished with her cool down after being on the treadmill, she couldn't believe who entered the gym. The one and only Stanley Lewis.

Stanley smiled and walked over to Jackie. "Good morning, Ms. Lewis. How did you sleep last night? You must have been really drunk."

"Look, Stanley. You stole my suite and I didn't appreciate it," Jackie said.

Stanley said, "That wasn't your suite."

"Boy, I'm not playing with you," she said.

"What are you going to do to me, Jackie? What the fuck can you do to possibly hurt me anymore than you already have? What are you going to do sleep with my friend? Oops, you already did that," Stanley said.

She mocked him with her response. "Stanley, I'm so sorry that you are still bitter."

He said, "If you are really sorry, bend over so I can hit that one last time."

Jackie replied, "Bitch, please. That will never happen."

Stanley said, "Oh, Jackie. It will happen. And when it does, you will be begging me not to stop."

Jackie sanitized the treadmill. Once she was done, Stanley patted her on her ass and then said, "Keep it tight for me, baby."

"Fuck you, Stanley!" Jackie yelled.

———————————

Eric rubbed his eyes as he slowly woke up. Nikki said, "Good morning, handsome."

"Oh man, baby. What time is it?" Eric asked.

Nikki said, "10:00a.m."

"Why did you let me sleep so long?"

"Well, Eric we aren't in our 30's anymore. I felt that as hard as you work when we are at home pulling twelve to sixteen hours a day, five to six days a week that you needed the rest. Plus, your work phone wasn't going off nor was your personal phone. Besides, I haven't watched you sleep since we were in high school, and it brought back lots of good memories."

"What memories did you have?" Eric asked.

Nikki said, "I remembered our very first time as well as when I lost our baby. A lot of good and bad, but our good outweighs our bad."

Eric said, "Do you love me the same, less, or more today from the first day that you met me?"

Nikki answered, "From the first day that I ever met you, I fell head over hills in love with you. However, today, I love you ten times more."

Eric said, "Can you hand me that book bag right there?" She gave it to him. "I wasn't for sure when I was going to do this or how, but today is the day."

He placed the bookbag on the floor by the bed and knelt down on one knee.

Nikki gasped. Eric unzipped his bag and pulled out a small jewelry box. He said, "I've loved you from the first day I've ever met you. I know that we have had our fair share of ups and downs, but I promised myself that I wouldn't ask you to marry me until I had over a million dollars in the bank. You deserve to have the same life as your friends. So, with that in mind, Nikki Stewart, will you marry me?"

He opened the box to reveal a ten-karat seamless, halo round stone diamond ring designed by Nikki's favorite jeweler, Jean Doussett. Tears are running down her eyes as she said, "YESSSSSS, Eric, YESSSSSSSS."

Nikki joined him on the floor and straddled him as they kissed passionately to commemorate the moment. She said, "Oh my God! It's beautiful. Does this mean that I must keep my promise and give you a baby?"

Eric said, "Nikki, sweetheart, that is totally up to you. I know you will be a great mom, so you make that decision."

"Let me get my phone. I need to call my mom and my sisters," she said.

"No need for that. They helped me design the ring. We've come a long way baby," Eric said.

—————————

Lisa said, "You didn't wake me up for 5a.m. prayer this morning."

Mark said, "I didn't want to wake you this morning. I needed to spend some time with God solo."

"Oh. Is everything ok, Mark?"

He chuckled and said, "Yes, Lisa. I just wanted to truly thank God for your forgiveness and true friendship with the gang. Yesterday couldn't have been better. Because of my position, I sometimes forget to relax and have fun. We danced, sang, and joked all night. You know Sam will be the next mayor, which will make us elevate because we are his church home. If he decides to run for governor or even the President of the United States, we will always be a part of that select few that will move with him."

Lisa ignored the last part of what Mark said. She wasn't concerned with elevation and status. Lisa just enjoyed spending some time with her husband and supporting her friends.

She said, "Last night was wonderful. I felt like we were back in college. Thank you for dancing with me."

"I can't do that all the time. It will always depends on who is in the room, but I will promise not to be so strict in the church. We had just as much fun last night without the drinking," he said.

"Would you like to order room service, or do you want to go down for breakfast?" she asked.

"Why don't you tie the red scarf on the door, and we'll talk about it in about an hour?" Mark said with a wink.

———————————

"Shonda, are you almost ready to go down for breakfast?"

"Almost Jerry. I'm just touching up my makeup." Shonda comes out in her Earnest Sewn blue jeans and an Earnest Sewn baby doll T-shirt.

"You look great in those jeans," Jerry said with admiration.

She said, "Thank you. This outfit cost me an entire paycheck."

Jerry asked, "What? Why would you spend that much on an outfit?"

Shonda explained. "I'm the poorest one in this group. The only reason they let me in is because my brother, Richard, is a doctor. Jackie and I have been friends ever since we were in grade school. I don't always want my friends to purchase things for me that I can't afford for myself"

"What you don't want is to be one of those women that can buy whatever they want, but have to beg for what they need from their man," Jerry said.

Shonda couldn't believe that the lie just rolled so effortlessly off her tongue. She took the money that London left and purchased this outfit. She hoped London ate his heart out after seeing her look so damn good.

Jerry interrupted her train of thought. He said, "When we get married, you won't have to worry about money anymore. It would be my responsibility to take care of you and supply all your needs and wants. However, you never answered me. "

She said, "I'm so sorry. I'm just not sure yet."

"Okay, that's fair. You didn't say no," Jerry said.

As Shonda and Jerry walked past Diane & London's room, they saw the red scarf on the door. She got emotional and wanted to burst into tears, but she remembered she just made love to Jerry last night. She grabbed Jerry's hand and pulled herself together. She would deal with London later.

———————————

Diane opened the curtains. "Rise and shine, party animal."

"Damn, are you trying to kill me with that sunlight?" London said.

"No. It is time to go downstairs for breakfast, sleepy head. How do you expect to win the girl if you don't get up to play the game?" Diane asked.

He said, "No, problem. Let me take a shower. By the way, what time is it?

She said, "About 10:30a.m."

Man, we will be having lunch instead of breakfast. I hope that's okay with you," London said.

"Breakfast, lunch, whatever. I'm hungry. Just hurry up, boy," Diane said.

He hurried to the shower and got dressed.

As they were on their way out, London noticed the red scarf on the door. He giggled. He said, "May I ask what this is about?" He touched the scarf. "I didn't get any from you last night, did I?"

"No, London. Didn't I say let me do this? I know what I'm doing. Just follow my lead. Now hold my hand as we walk into the dining room."

———————————

"Sam, are you done with your morning calls?" Peace asked.

"Yes, my queen. Let's go."

As Peace and Sam headed to the banquet room, they noticed all of the red scarves on the doors. Peace nudged Sam, and they giggled. He said, "Thank God most of our friends can no longer bear children."

Peace said, "How do you know that? Men and women have been known to conceive a child during their late 40's or the early part of their 50's. "

He said, "Anyone that chooses to have a child that late in life, God bless their hearts."

_____

Richard said, "Let's go. I'm hungry."

Velma said, "Give me five minutes. I'm trying to get my hair together especially since we are going horseback riding today."

Richard rolled his eyes. "Who cares what your hair looks like?"

Velma replied, "I do. I don't want your friend, Jackie, staring at me and thinking that she looks better than everyone."

"Please don't start with that Jackie stuff. You are my wife. I love you, okay," Richard reassured Velma.

She said, "Sure, I'm so sorry, Richard. Let's go."

"Look, Velma all I ever wanted in life was a wife and possibly a kid or two. I hope that's enough for you. Your insecurity about Jackie is starting to drive me crazy. This is how a perfect love can start to go wrong," Richard said.

"I know Richard. I'm sorry," she said.

As they left the room, he said, "By the way, you look GREAT, Velma."

Velma said nothing as they headed to the banquet hall.

MORNING ANNOUNCEMENTS

Sam, Peace, and Tim walked into the banquet hall. They were laughing and reminiscing about last night. Gina waved at them as they made their way toward her.

"Good morning, my beautiful sister-in-law," Sam said.

Gina said, "Good morning, Sam and Tim. Hey, big sis."

Peace greeted her sister with a kiss on the cheek. "Good morning, my love. Come on, guys. Let's go to the buffet and eat. The food looks great."

She led the way, followed by Sam, then Tim and Gina. While in line, Gina tapped Tim on the shoulder and asked him, "What's your last name, again?"

"It's Ross. Why do you ask, Gina?"

"Well, Tim, I believe I have a right to know what my new last name would be." She winked as she placed food on to her plate.

Tim blushed and said, "Well, I guess you do."

Several others sat together and started eating.

Jerry said, "Good morning, Pastor and First Lady Taylor. May we join you?"

Mark said, "Man, Deacon, please do before we get a cussing bandit or talking Annie here. It will be our pleasure."

Lisa said, "Shonda, you look so pretty this morning."

"Thank you, Lisa."

Jerry said, "Go ahead. Tell her what type of jeans you have on."

Shonda said, "Jerry! Lisa don't care."

"Yes, Lisa do. Who are you wearing?" Lisa asked.
She said, "Ok, it's an Earnest Sewn outfit!" Lisa and Shonda screamed at the table.

"Ladies, we are at the table."

"Sorry, Pastor. . . oops, Mark," Shonda said.
Lisa asked, "Did Jackie purchase that outfit for you?"

"Nope, Lisa. I paid for it all by myself."

"Good for you, Shonda. You look even better now that I know who you are wearing."

"Lisa, brand names don't make you look better," Jerry said.

She said, "It just enhances your soul to help you strut with confidence."

Mark said, "Jerry, you will not win when it comes to money with this group of women. Let's eat. I'm headed to the carving station. Lisa, you go to the salad bar. Because I don't want to hear you whining Monday that you gained two pounds."

Everyone laughed but Lisa. She knew her husband was dead serious.

Shonda said, "Come on, Lisa. I'll hit the salad bar with you. I can barely breathe in these jeans."

Lisa said, "Thanks, Shonda. Jackie and Barry are coming in. They can sit at the table next to us."

Jackie greeted them. "Hey, girls. Did everyone enjoy their night?"

Shonda answered quickly, "Yes, Jackie. I surely did."
Jackie arched her eyebrows and asked, "You got something you want to share with the group? I see you in that Earnest Sewn outfit. You are looking quite amazing today, I must say."

"Good morning ladies. Jackie, I'm going to grab us that table right next to them, so you ladies can continue to talk," Barry said.

Lisa apologized to him. "Where are our manners? It's only been about eight hours since we have last seen each other."

Barry waved his hand as he headed to the line. "I have been around you ladies long enough to know not to take it personal."

Jackie said, "Okay, y'all. Since Barry is gone, I can talk. We did it last night."

They all screamed. Peace excused herself from the table with her group and headed towards them. She said, "Girls, what is all this noise about?"

Shonda said, "Jackie, tell Peace or I will."

"Barry and I made love last night," Jackie said.

"And Jerry and I did, too." Shonda said.

Then Peace started screaming. The other girls joined because they had just found out about Shonda and Jerry, too.

Just then London walked up and said, "Ladies, what are we all excited about?"

Shonda said, "Nothing, London. How was your night last night?" Diane replied, "It was great. Thank you for asking." She grabbed London's hand. "Come on. Stanley and Tara have invited us to sit with them."

Shonda replied, "Tramp." The girls screamed again.

Now everyone was in the buffet lines. While in line, London stood behind Shonda.

"Damn, you surely look good in those jeans," he said.

"I'm glad you like them London because you paid for them," Shonda said.

"So, Shonda, if I paid for them, does this mean that I can get in them with you?"

"No, London, it doesn't. You were all in Diane's last night. Go back to her."

He said, "Did you forget I bust that cherry, and I have a picture to prove it?"

She said, "You better not have a picture."

"You know me better than that. Look when we get home tomorrow night, I'll be over there. Just wear those jeans and a sexy red bra only. I'll take care of the rest," London said.

Shonda said, "I'm here with Jerry, and he may want to make love to me again."

London replied, "You will only be thinking about me. Compare who is the best. I already know that I'll win hands down and tongue out. Love you, boo."

Damn it. How could Shonda hate someone so much, but she couldn't get him off her mind. If Shonda would be honest with herself, she would admit the truth. London was right. Shonda bit a piece of her bacon and wondered if she did have that red bra as she joined Jerry at their table.

Nikki said to Jackie, "May we sit with you and Barry?"

"Sure, we are sitting at the table next to Mark and Lisa," she said.

"Great. Eric, sit your backpack in the chair. I'll head to the omelet station," Nikki said.

Nikki and Peace greeted each other.

Peace said, "Why are you and Eric so late getting down here?"

"Do you want the long or short version?" Nikki held up her hand.

Peace screamed. Jackie, Lisa, and Shonda ran over to them. They all screamed, "Oh my God!"

Mark said, "Eric, what is that all about?"

Eric said, "That's about the ten-carat, custom made Jean Doussett ring that I placed on Nikki's left hand this morning."

Jerry said, "Let me be the first to congratulate you & Nikki." He hoped that Shonda would accept his marriage proposal.

Eric said, "Thanks, Jerry. It's been long overdue."

Mark said, "Better late than never, if you truly love her."

"I've always loved her, but for years, she challenged everything I did. However, once we quit trying to make each other into someone else and truly loved each other for who we are, it is amazing. She respects my opinions, and I respect her. Now we are tighter than ever before," Eric explained.

Mark said, "Well, I'll be the second to congratulate you. When is the big day?"

Eric said, "You know that's up to her and the girls. I have no control over that. I'm hoping that we can go to an island with all our close friends plus family and call it a day."

Mark and Jerry both said, "Good luck with that one, Eric."

Meanwhile, the girls pressed for more details about Nikki's engagement.

Jackie said, "When did this happen?"

"This morning," Nikki said.

"Let me see your ring." Nikki held up her hand. Jackie said, "Is this a Marc Jacob or a Jean Doussett?"

Nikki replied, "JD, of course."

Shonda said, "Your ring is gorgeous."

Nikki said, "Thank you, but damn you look good your damn self."

Jackie said, "That's because Shonda has a surprise for you as well,"
"Jackie!" Shonda screamed.

She spilled the beans. "Shonda got laid last night."

"By whom?" Nikki asked.

Lisa said, "Nikki, what do you mean? She's in love with Jerry."

"Not really. London is still in the running," Nikki said.

"London is out of the picture," Shonda said.

Peace quieted the girls down. "Ladies, shhh, stop. I adore both of them. We will have a lot to discuss when we return home."

The ladies laughed and continued to their stations of choice before returning to their tables.

"Peace, what was all the racket with you and the girls? Sam asked.

"Nikki and Eric are now engaged, and Shonda is in love. This is so exciting!" Peace said.

Sam said, "Wow! Only an Evans event can do that, baby."

Gina said, "I'm so happy for Nikki and Eric. Love is definitely in the air."

Peace said, "Well, you should know."

"What does that mean?" Gina asked.

"I see the way you are looking at Tim," Peace answered.

"Peace! How am I looking at Tim? Gina said.
"With goo-goo eyes." Peace said. Gina wasn't the only one checking him out.

Sam said, "Peace, can you please stand with me?"

Sam asked for everyone's attention. He said, "As most of you know, we have been hosting an after-weekend getaway for as long as my wife has been having a birthday party fundraiser gala. Throughout the years, it has continued to grow."

He motioned for Eric and Nikki to join him. They stood beside him.

Sam continued, "Nevertheless, interesting things happen each yea. But this year has become the most exciting. One of my very best friends has finally proposed to his beautiful girlfriend. I know her girls have congratulated her, but please let us all raise our glasses to salute Eric Ramsey & Nikki Stewart. Maybe next year, we'll be hosting a wedding up here."

The crowd became excited while clanging their knives against their glasses. Eric and Nikki engaged in a passionate kiss. Then Nikki modeled the Jean Doussett ring for everyone again.

Eric turned to Sam and said, "Thank you and your lovely wife. We love you, man. Frat for life!"

FUN TIME

Everyone gathered at the stables where the horses and four-wheelers were located. Several guests took guided horseback rides and a hayride. They also went apple-picking and four-wheeling in the forest.

As Jackie and the girls finished up with horseback riding, Jackie's private phone rang.

Peace said in disappointment, "Jackie, you know the rules. No business phone calls while we are on vacation."

Jackie said, "You know that my business phone is off. This is my emergency cell phone. It's Kelly, my assistant." The phone continued to ring as if the person demanded that the call be answered immediately. Jackie pressed the green button and said, "Hey, Kelly. What's up?"

"Hello Ms. Stewart. I am so sorry to bother you, but by any chance is Stanley with you all this weekend?" she asked.

"Yes, Kelly, he is. What is going on?" Jackie said.

She said, "The hospital just called here looking for you or Stanley. Ms. Stewart, I am sorry to inform you that his mom has passed away. My condolences to you and Stanley."

Jackie screamed, "Oh my God! Oh my God!"

Peace asked in a concerned voice, "What is wrong?"

"Stanley's mother just died," Jackie replied quietly with tears streaming down her face.

"Oh, Jackie. I am so sorry. I know how close you all were," Peace said as she comforted her.

Jackie tried to steady her voice. "Kelly, thank you so much for the call. I will let Stanley know. Then we will call his family. I do not know if he will be up to driving home today or tomorrow as planned. Have a good day."
Jackie put the private phone back in her pocket. She said, "Ladies, I need to find Barry and speak to him."

Lisa said "He is over there with Mark."

Jackie said, "Thanks Lisa. I will be right back."

She approached the men as they seemed to be engaged in a pleasant conversation. Barry fit in so well with their group. It was like he had always been there. She waited for a minute, but both men looked up and saw the tears flowing down her face.

She said, "Excuse me. Barry, may I speak to you privately for a moment please?"

Barry said, "Why sure, Jackie. Excuse us, Mark."

They walked a little distance before he asked, "Jackie, what's wrong?"

She said, "I have a family emergency, and I need to speak to Stanley privately. Will that be okay with you?"

He said, "Sure, Jackie. Is everything okay? Is there anything that I can do for you?"

"Stanley's mom just passed away. Can you keep Tara company while I inform Stanley?" Jackie said.

He kissed her and said, "Sure, my love, anything for you."

Barry and Jackie approached them after they just shared an intimate hug and laugh.

Jackie said, "Stanley, may I speak with you privately for a minute please?"

Stanley said, "Tara, excuse us, please." Jackie and Stanley walked towards the ranch house.

Tara said, "Barry, do you know what that is all about?"

"Some type of family emergency," Barry said.

"I hope everything is well with their kids. This is the hardest part about dating a divorced man that still shares friends with his ex-wife," Tara said.

Barry said, "That's so true. I have to see Stanley everywhere Jackie and I go."

"What have we gotten ourselves into? I think we need a drink." Tara and Barry laughed.

"Do you want to hear my diagnosis?" he said.

"Give it to me straight, Doc," she said.

Barry said, "We're crazy in love. The heart wants what the heart wants."

"Talk, sir. I think mimosas are in order," Tara said.

―――――――――――――

Stanley said, "I knew you were going to run back and beg sooner than later. Make it a quickie because my woman will want some more later. "

Jackie entered his cabin while shaking her head. That foolishness didn't even deserve a response.

Stanley placed his hand around her waist and gazed into her eyes. "Damn, Jackie. Why did you have to fuck up my fairytale life? I still love you, but I hate the way you broke up our family."

"I have told you several times how sorry I am. I am so sorry that I could not love you the way that you deserved to be loved. I am so sorry that I ruined your fairytale life. I can't change what I did."

She rested her forehead against his. "One thing will not change, Stanley. We will always be family, which is why I need to speak with you." She paused for a moment. Then Jackie said quietly, "Mommy passed away this morning."

Stanley stumbled to the bed, stunned. He said, "What, my mommy?"

Jackie and Stanley cried together for about fifteen minutes. She said, "I am so sorry, but we need to call the hospital."

"Can you call them for me? I cannot talk right now," Stanley whispered.

Jackie got Dr. Wilkes on the line. "This is Jackie & Stanley Lewis calling on behalf of Bernice Lewis. "

Dr. Wilkes said, "My condolences to you and your family."

"What happened?" Stanley asked.

"Your mother chose hospice care about two months ago," Dr. Wilkes explained.
Stanley said, "What? Doctor Wilkes, my mom knew she was dying and said nothing! Is my dad there?"

Dr. Wilkes said, "Yes, he was right by her side. Your sister, Niecy was just notified as well by the hospice social worker. She will be here by Monday."

Stanley broke down and cried harder. It hurt him that he missed his mother's final moments. He felt like he was not a good son.

Dr. Wilkes comforted him. "Stanley, it is honorable of your mother not to include others in her private moment. Most people do it because they are okay with transitioning. They have chosen to allow God to come when it is their time."

Jackie grabbed some tissues and wiped away his tears. She kissed his forehead and held his hand. Stanley cleared his throat and said, "I am not surprised. My mother has always been secretive. Thank you for being there for her."

Dr. Wilkes said, "No problem. If you know your mom, then you know everything is already in place including her obituary, her repast location, the food, and her services. The funeral is set for this Wednesday."

Stanley chuckled. "Yes, that is my mom. I am sure everything will be perfect. She would not have it any other way."

"I will transfer you to the social worker now. Please feel free to reach out to hospice if you or your family need anything," Dr. Wilkes said.

Stanley finished up with the social worker, then he and Jackie reached out to his dad, Fred and his sister, Niecy. Afterwards, Stanley grabbed Jackie's hand and passionately kissed her, and she did not resist.

With their shirts unbuttoned, Jackie and Stan's flame reignited for a moment. For a moment, Jackie moaned as Stanley found her sweet spot in the middle of her collarbone. For a moment, Stanley fumbled with the button on her jeans and anticipated to come home again. And then her lovemaking session with Barry flashed across her mind. Jackie backed Stanley off of her.

She said, "Stanley, you know that you were wrong for that."

He replied, "You enjoyed that. Sympathy had nothing to do with what just went down. You need to quit playing and let me hit that real quick."

"Hmm. How soon you forget about your little Tara." Jackie fixed her clothes and hair. "My man is waiting on me."

"Alright, mama. Service is Wednesday, and I will be spending the night at my mansion that I paid for," Stanley said.

"With whom?"

"My wife."

"Your *ex*-wife."

Stanley patted her on the ass. "Whatever you say, Jackie. I am man enough to wait until you get through playing around with every Richard, Barry, and Michael. You will realize that—"

He lowered the bass in his voice and crooned in Barry White style, "You will never-ever find—"

Jackie opened the door and pushed him out. "Let's go, Romeo."

Stanley stumbled, but kept on singing. "A man to love you like I do." Jackie rolled her eyes and laughed as they rejoined the group.

Barry and Tara gave each other knowing looks as Stanley and Jackie walked up to the bar. Stanley kissed Tara then brought her up to speed with what had just taken place. Well, not everything.

Then he joined the fellas and shared everything with them. Mark informed Stanley that he got the call at about 6a.m. this morning and had sent his assistant, Pastor Greg Robinson to be with his parents. Mark had known for several weeks that she was in hospice. As a shepherd to his congregation, Mark could never betray anyone's confidentiality.

Stanley said, "You know, Mark, that is the one reason why we are still your members. Even when it hurts like hell, we know that we can always trust you. Thanks, man."

"You have my deepest condolences. I love you, and I will continue to pray for you and your family." He shook Stanley's hand and embraced him.

Stanley pushed back his tears. "Thank you, Pastor Mark. Please pray that Jackie and I get back together. It is moments like these that let you know how much people really mean to you."

Mark said, "What does Jackie want?"

"The way she just kissed me. The way we almost made love a few minutes ago. I know she still wants me. Jackie is madly in love with me, man. I never stopped loving her," Stanley confided.

Eric chimed in as the voice of reason. "What about Barry, man? Do you think maybe she kissed you because of the circumstances? Grief can make you draw closer to people in that moment."

Stanley replied, "Sam, you know more than anyone about me and Jackie's relationship."

Sam said, "You guys bring *way* too much excitement to my life. I do not miss the drama. Peace and I are in a good place. You and Jackie apparently had problems."

"We didn't have problems until other people came into her life and told her that she had problems," Stanley said as he looked directly at Richard.

Eric said, "Damn, Stanley, that's deep."

Stanley said, "Deep, but true. People have no problem pointing out all the faults in your relationship while secretly wanting what you have."

Sam said, "All I can tell you is to think about the other people that you will be hurting like Tara."

Stanley said, "I will, but life is too short to live with regret. I am not saying that we will be back together tomorrow, but if it is God's will. I really miss having my wife and family."

He poked Eric in his chest. "Think about all you and Nikki went through. What if you were in my position right now? What if you got the opportunity to win her back? Wouldn't you take the chance?"

Eric gazed at Nikki. "Most definitely, man, but it's not that simple. You and Jackie—"

Stanley got in Sam's face. "Frat to frat, man. Peace left you for all the hell you put her through. You fought for her. Keep it 100, man."

Sam squared his jaw. He and Peace were definitely not like Jackie and Stan. His frat had to consider what drove them apart in the first place before Jackie's affair began. But Sam also knew what it meant to face the possibility of not having the woman he truly loved in his life.

He said, "You're right, Stan."

"Then fellas, tell me. What's a man supposed to do?"

———————————

"Thank you for being so understanding and keeping Tara company for me," Jackie said.

Barry said, "No problem. Tara and I just talked about leaving you and Stanley here and running off to get married. We are both aware that you two have unfinished business."

Jackie hit Barry's shoulder. "Were we gone that long?"

"Exactly 1 hour and 43 minutes. Is he going home tonight?"

"We found out that his mom had been in hospice for a couple of months and arranged everything herself. Barry, she even did her own obituary."

He said, "Damn, that was very brave of her, Jackie."

"Mommy was that type of woman. We called the kids, his sister and dad, plus everyone else about the services that will be held this Wednesday afternoon," Jackie said.

"Then I know where you will be."

"Yes, Barry. We are still family."

"Absolutely, Jackie."

"I need to let my girls know what has taken place," she said.

He said, "Go ahead. I am on my way to speak with London."

————————————

"How is it going with you, man?" Barry said.

"It would be going better if I were with Shonda," London said.

He said, "How did she wind up here with dude?"

London replied, "Her best friend, Lisa is pushing the good old deacon on her. Man, the sad part is I know she wants me bad."

Barry said, "If she genuinely wants you, you will make sure that we all know it eventually." They both shook hands and laughed. "What are you going to do about Diane?"

London said, "She checked me before we got here. After Peace's party, she told me that she knows that I am in love with Shonda. If I let her control this weekend, I'll have Shonda back my way real soon. It was her idea to put the red scarf on the door, and it worked. Shonda keeps whispering about it to me." Barry laughed. "Shonda is taken right now."

"No, she's not. Shonda is a much right girl."

"What, London? A much right girl!"

"Yes, Barry. Shonda ain't married, so she is a much right girl. I got as much right to her as he does."

Barry laughed again. "Man, you are crazy."

Stanley then walked over to where they were. "What are you guys laughing about?"

"Nothing, man. My condolences to you and your family," Barry said as he left London and Stanley alone.

"Thanks, Barry."

London looked confused. Stanley said, "My mother passed away today."

"Oh, I'm so sorry. Let me know if it is anything that I can do for you and your family," London said.

Stanley said, "Just you being there is good enough for me. You are truly the only one that knows what I'm going through, and I'm not talking about with my mom."

London said, "I know how it is to see the woman you love hugging another man. That shit hurts like hell."

Stanley said, "I know, right."

JACKIE AND THE GIRLS

Nikki said, "How did Stanley handle the news?"

Jackie said, "We cried together for about fifteen to twenty minutes. It was so sad. She had been in hospice and never shared that she was dying with anyone, but her husband. None of his family members were aware, not even his sister."

Lisa said, "I am so sorry. Mark and I knew. We have been ministering to them. I helped her with the obituary and everything. Her repast is going to be at E's Place. You know how she was about keeping the money in the family. It is all paid for and everything."

Jackie said, "You could have told me, Lisa."

Shonda said, "Jackie, don't do that. You know that she could not tell you. She is a co-pastor as well as the first lady."

"I know. I just would have wanted to be there with her," Jackie began to cry. The girls surrounded her with love.

———————

The cowbell began to ring. The host called Sam up to the mic. Sam said, "We will continue with a big barbecue and a campfire at dusk. Today has been quite interesting. We lost a core member of our family. Mama Lewis has gone to be with the Lord, so let us have a moment of silence."

After everyone observed the moment of silence, Sam asked them to keep Stanley and Jackie in their prayers as well as the entire Lewis family. Stanley thanked Sam. After Pastor Mark blessed the food, everyone scattered to different buffet lines.

Nikki said to Jackie, "Which direction did our men go?"
"I have no idea, but we better start at the salad buffet first. I barely worked out this morning," she said.

Nikki said, "Eric and I got our sexercise on this morning. I know we burnt off about 2500 calories."

Jackie said, "So did Barry and me, however, that did not stop me from kissing Stanley today."

"What!"

"Nikki, do not judge me. I do not know why I let him kiss me. He was talking all kind of shit on the way to his cabin before I informed him of Mommy's death. Then when I told him. he cried and I cried, and then he kissed me. I did not stop him. I felt like I did when we were in college. We would have made love if I did not stop him."

"Jackie, that is serious. Are you sure you and Stanley are over?"

She said, "No, Nikki. I am not. I feel like I am in love with him all over again. What am I going to do?"

Nikki said, "I have no idea. But I do know one thing."

Jackie asked, "What is that?"

"Better you than me. Whichever man you choose, I will still love them and you."

Nikki and Jackie laughed as they carried their plates to their table where Eric and Barry were waiting for them.

———————

Tim asked Gina, "Is it always this much fun here?"

She said, "Yes. They used to bring the in-laws and the kids, but now that everyone is older and doing their own thing, it's pretty much all adult couples."

Tim said, "Well, we are not a couple."

"Not yet. If you play your cards right, we just might become one."

———————

Tara asked Stanley. "How are you feeling?"

"I'm okay for now. Thank you for asking," Stanley said.

"I noticed that Sam sent out condolences to both you and Jackie," Tara said.

"She is the mother of my kids and she was my wife for over twenty years. My parents know her only as a daughter," Stanley said with contention.

Tara said, "I am so sorry. I did not mean to upset you. I do realize that she will always be like family."

Stanley clenched his teeth and said, "No, she *is* family." He angrily moved toward the buffet stations.

London complimented Shonda again at the meat table. She laughed while she fixed her plate. He continued to flirt with her. "I cannot wait until tomorrow night."

Shonda said, "None for you tomorrow if I see that red scarf tonight."

"You mean you really want to see me tomorrow, Shonda?"

"Sort of, London."

"Then tell me you love me," he said.

She said, "You know that I do."

London said, "Then why are you here with dude?"

"We will discuss it tomorrow." Shonda walked away.

As Shonda joined the group, Lisa said, "What were you two laughing about at the buffet?"

"You know London is crazy. He is always saying something," she said.

Lisa replied, "That's because he is stupid."

Mark said, "Now that is not first lady like, is it?"

Lisa apologized. "No, it is not. I'm sorry about speaking that way about your friend."

"She's got a point, Mark. He is immature," Jerry said.

"Why would you say that?" Shonda asked.

"Because it is true. He knows that we are here together, and he is disrespectful to both Diane and me," Jerry said.

Shonda said, "London is my friend just like these good people who are sitting with us. He helped me get out of my shell. Believe it or not, he taught me how to be a woman. He brought me out of my shyness and told me all day long that I was as sexy as every woman in this group. He gave me confidence that I never had."

Those words hurt Jerry. He thought that he made her feel very much like a sexy woman last night. Was it even worth it to keep competing for her affection?

Jerry said, "I didn't know that your *friend* knew you so well."

Shonda said, "It is a lot about me you don't know. If you had met me four or five years ago, you would not be interested in me at all. I am who I am today because of him."

Mark said, "I hope that I have never given you the impression that I do not like London because I do."

Shonda said, "I am sorry. I was not directing that at you, just the other two."

Lisa and Jerry remained quiet. Each of them still did not like London.

To Lisa, any man who kept talking about sex wasn't serious about a commitment. But what did she know? She dealt with Mark's negative treatment of her because she must admit that she loved status and fashion more.

To Jerry, any man who is that intimately involved in a woman's life wasn't just a friend. He still wanted to marry her, though. She had his heart.

Mark said, "Okay, let's quit harassing Shonda about her friend. We all have people in our lives that other people do not care for."

Shonda said, "Thank you, Pastor."

His voice of correction made Lisa drop her head, while Jerry apologized for the both of them.

Jerry said, "Our goal was never meant to hurt your feelings. London is your friend, and we need to respect that." He rubbed Shonda's knee under that table.

After dinner, everyone gathered around the barn fire. The group continued to enjoy stories, roast marshmallows, and make smores until it was time to return to their cabins.

BACK HOME

The concierge put everyone's luggage on the coach bus as the group enjoyed their final buffet breakfast together. Stanley ran inside the room and spoke to everyone before he whispered in Jackie's ear.

He said, "I really need you. I will meet you at our home tomorrow then we can discuss my mom's service. May I come by?"

She said, "Sure, call me when you are on your way. Drive safely."

When Stanley walked off, Barry asked Jackie, "What was that all about?"

"He needs my assistance with his mother's service."

"I thought that she had taken care of everything herself, Jackie."

"Yes, Barry. She did the preliminaries. However, since he asked me for my help, that is what family is for."

He said, "Family? Jackie, you divorced that man. Besides, isn't he a big-time attorney?"

Jackie said, "I can't believe your behavior right now."

"Damn it Jackie. You don't see it. Your husband will do anything to get you back. But that's not his fault," Barry said angrily.

"Don't be like that, Barry. His mother just died. Whose fault is it?"

Barry said, "Partially, your fault. You never put him in his place. I will tell you this. Please don't invite me anywhere else that I have to deal with him."

Jackie said, "We can discuss this later."

Barry said, "The subject is not up for discussion anymore."

———————

Sam said, "Good morning everyone. We want to thank everyone for a wonderful, fabulous, and exciting weekend. This weekend will go down in history for the Evans family. Nothing here was scripted, just a ton of fun. We are asking that you go to the restrooms before you board the bus. I don't know if we have any games on the way home. I believe we are all so tired that we will be sleep within thirty minutes of pulling off."
"Nikki yelled out, "No games!"

Sam said, "Thank you, the future Mrs. Ramsey. Ok, let's go."

During the six-hour trip, everyone was either sleeping, posting on social media, checking work emails, or making small talk with their partners. When they made it back to E's Place, Sam and Peace thanked everyone and took up a collection for the bus driver. They gathered their belongings and got off the bus.

EXITING THE BUS

As the girls finished making plans for dinner tomorrow night, Richard offered his condolences to Jackie. He asked Jackie to keep him and Velma updated on the details of the service.

As Shonda said her goodbyes to Lisa, she walked towards the car where Jerry was waiting for her. London called her name, and she stopped.

"What's up London?"

"Just a reminder, I'll be over there around 8:00p.m."

"Okay, London. Would you like dinner?" Shonda said.

He said, "No, just you."

Shonda giggled as she finally reached Jerry's car. He asked, "What is so funny?"

She said, "Nothing I'm laughing at London."

"Oh, go figure. . ."

_____

"Eric, lift this suitcase for me."

"Nikki, we were only gone for the weekend. Why did you have to pack all this shit anyway? You did not even wear half of it."

She said, "If you must know, I was not sure how I would be feeling."

He said, "You are crazy. We must make a stop by my mom's house on the way home."

Nikki asked, "Why?"

Eric replied, "She wants to see your ring. They are so excited. She said that it was about time."

"I agree with your mom," Nikki said.

"Have you spoken with your family yet?"

"Hell, no. They would have started planning the wedding before we got home. I'll go over there tomorrow after the girls and I talk about it."

Eric said, "Really, Nikki. Do I have any say so in this?"

Nikki said, "Yes. The budget. How much do we want to spend on this wedding?"

"I thought the bride's parents are supposed to pay for the wedding."

"Eric, my family do not have that type of money."

"I don't know. I don't want to go broke having an extravagant wedding, Nikki."

"Eric, I am worth it."

"Yes, you are. But let's be practical. We must live afterwards," he said.

Nikki said, "How about this? I will match whatever you put in."

Eric said, "How about $5,000?"

Nikki said, "$20,000."

"Hell, no. $10,000. That's my final offer, or we are going to the White Chapel in Vegas."

"Ok, Eric, but you know that you are not the boss of me."

———————————

Mark said, "How many times do I have to tell you that as the first lady of my congregation that you are not entitled to render your opinion of others? We must be incredibly careful of prejudiced reviews. We can NOT ever comment on other religions, politics, sexual preferences, or people, period. It is our only our job to spread the word of God's love for Shonda, Jerry, and London, and the world. I don't ever want to tell you that again. Do you understand me?"

Lisa said, "Yes, I'm so sorry if I embarrassed you."

Mark said, "You didn't embarrass me. People will look at you as an untrained first lady. Now other than that situation, did you have fun?"

Lisa said, "Yes. I am extremely excited for Nikki and Eric and sad for Stanley and Jackie."

"You see, Lisa, this is why we don't take sides. I love Stanley, and now Jackie is with Barry. He's a cool brother as well, but don't be surprised if something like this brings Jackie and Stanley back together. If that should happen, I would still be friends with Barry."

"Oh, I truly do see what you are saying, Mark. I will never do that again."

Peace said, "You sure do host some of the most exciting and unpredictable events in the world."

"Is that right? I do know that some of these friends belong to you as well," Sam said.

"Perhaps two, maybe three of them." Peace laughed. "I had a ball, but I surely believed that by time we arrived at the ranch that there was going to be a fight between Jackie and Stanley or London and Jerry. I think I'm jealous that no one has ever wanted to fight over me."

Sam giggled and said, "Peace, I will beat someone down to the ground for you. Just for the record, there are a plenty of men and women out there that would love to step to you. They just know you have 250 pounds of sexiness that they can't come close to comparison."

Peace laughed hysterically as she pinched his excess stomach fat. Her laughs grew louder and louder until they became infectious. Sam joined her with tears streaming down his eyes. He knew he might need to hit the gym a little more, but hey, a brother was still *fine*.

Sam said, "Control yourself. You are so crazy. However, I do agree that our weekend started out crazy, but ended with joy and pain. I'm so happy for Eric and Nikki, confused on Shonda,

Jerry and London, and sad for Stanley, Jackie, and Barry. I want to see how these triangles are going to end up in the future."

Peace said, "It's a tangled web that our friends are going to have to fix themselves. I'm just glad that it is just the two of us."

She pulled out her notebook and said, "I have to write down all of my questions that I need answered at our after-dinner meeting tomorrow. I'll keep you posted."

THE TANGLED WEB WE WEAVE

"Thank you, Stanley. It has been an interesting weekend. I'm truly sorry to hear about your mom."

"Tara, I must apologize to you. I know that you realized by now that I am not over my ex-wife. This lady is still controlling every aspect of my life. Even though I try to move on, I can't. I really want my wife back."

She said, "I am not stupid. After all, I did make partner in our firm. I knew that you wanted your wife back. Hell, after this weekend, I know that she is feeling the same way. But you two are bringing other people in your mess, and that is not right. I felt so sorry for Barry when she was consoling you during your time of need. That wasn't right for you all to leave for that length of time. Both of you disregarded your significant others." Stanley said, "Wait, just a minute. We were unaware of my mother's illness. It was a shock to both of us."

Tara said, "Well, shame on you that you didn't keep up with your parents and what was going on. I call my parents every week and fly home quite often to attend their doctor's appointments with them."

Stanley said, "It was my mother's choice to keep her illness away from me. You know what, Tara? You are right. Shame on me, but do you think that I have a chance to get Jackie back?"

Tara said, "OMG. Stanley, goodbye. You figure it out." She got out of his car and slammed the car door.

Stanley said, "Bye, bitch."

"Diane, thank you for understanding my situation with Shonda," London said.

She said, "I did not appreciate being used for my good looks. However, it does not take a rocket scientist to see how much you love Shonda. If she gives you a chance, she will be a lucky girl."

London said, "I truly thank you for that. I am going to give it my all because I am madly in love with her."

"Barry, I enjoyed you hanging out with me this weekend."

"Really, Jackie. I have imagined making love to you for the past year. Unlike most men, I am very selective about giving myself to women. I feel that when you decide to make love to a woman, it should be someone that you potentially see yourself with in the future."

She said, "What are you feeling about me now?"

He said, "I feel that you have unresolved issues with your ex-husband. You need to decide if you want him back before you bring anyone else in this nonsense. "

"So, what are you saying Barry?"

"Let me know what you want to do, Jackie. The ball is in your court. I will not wait forever."

———————————

Later that evening, London arrived at Shonda's condo and pushed the buzzer.

Shonda said, "Who is it?"

"It is the love of your life, girl. It is me, London."

Shonda opened the door dressed in a sexy, red lace bra on and her Earnest Sewn blue jeans. "Hey, big daddy," she said.

He said, "You wore what I asked of you. Thank you, ma. Shonda, I love you. Seeing you with someone else is driving me crazy. I cannot handle it."

Shonda said, "Don't do me like that. You were with Diane. I saw the red scarf on the door."

London laughed. "How did you feel when you saw the scarf? Were you jealous?"

"A little, but I didn't go out of my way to make Diane uncomfortable," Shonda said.

London said, "If you called her right now, she would tell you that I did not sleep with her because she knew that I was in love with you. It was her idea to put the scarf on the door to get a reaction out of you. And it worked. Come over here, baby. I don't care about the Deacon or Diane right now. I threw my bags down and raced over here to be with you."

Shonda said, "I love you, too." They spent the remainder of the evening making passionate love.

DINNER WITH THE GIRLS

As always, Shonda and Jackie get to the table first.

Shonda said, "Hey Jackie, what are you drinking?"

Jackie said, "I'm drinking a glass of 787 Chateau Margaux. Would you like to try a little?"

She said, "Is it sweet, Jackie?"

"No, this is a real wine. It is a Cabernet Sauvignon from a private selection. Taste it," she said.

"This is strong," Shonda said.

"It is what grown women drink," Jackie said.

"Can I talk to you in confidence?" she asked.

"Sure."

Shonda hesitated. Then she said, "I slept with London the night of Peace's birthday party, then Jerry the night of the dinner, and then London again last night. I think I am a whore. This is what I get for always talking about Nikki." Shonda began to cry.

Jackie said, "What the hell are you crying for? It is about time that you had your choice of men. Are you thinking about settling down with either one?"

Shonda said, "I want them both."

Jackie laughed. "Welcome to my world. But sweetie, you cannot handle two men at one time, or can you? I'm not here to judge you."

Shonda said, "No, I'm feeling guilty now."

"Which one do you want?" Jackie asked.

She replied, "Lisa wants me to choose Jerry, but London turns me on when he acts like a school jock."

Jackie replied, "You are a grown woman that must make this decision yourself. However, whomever you choose, I'm here for you."

"Thanks, Jackie. Please don't tell the other girls."
"Shonda, I will never discuss your personal business with anyone. Shhhh. . .the girls are walking in."

The ladies greeted each other. Nikki was the last one to come in. "I'm here. The finally engaged woman is here."

They all screamed. "Tell us how he proposed."

Nikki said, "I let him sleep in that morning because my fiancé work so many long hours that I just wanted him to rest."

Lisa said, "Ladies, did everyone hear that? Her fiancé."

Shonda said, "We heard it. Go ahead and finish talking about your fiancé." They all laughed.

Nikki said, "Where did I stop before I was so rudely interrupted? Okay, he wanted to know why I let him sleep so long, and then we had some small talk. I told him that I loved him. He asked me if I loved him the same, less, or more than when we started. My reply was ten times more, so he asked me to hand him his book bag. When I did, he went in the bag, got down on one knee, and asked me to marry him."

She flashed her ring. "And I said, YESSSSSSSS!"

"Congratulations!" They all shouted in excitement.

Jackie said, "Are we doing a destination wedding or E's Place?"

Nikki said, "I'm not sure yet. Eric doesn't want to spend more than $20,000 on the wedding."

"$20,000? My everyday Mercedes was $47,000, at least," Peace said.

Jackie said, "I know women that have spent $100,000 on a wedding and the marriage did not last a year."

Nikki said "That's true, too, Jackie."

Lisa said, "Nikki, put the time in the marriage. It will follow up with love, peace, and everlasting happiness."

Shonda changed the conversation. "So, how is your sex life with Eric? Does he still drive you KOO-KOO for COCO PUFFS as you used to say?"

Everyone was shocked that Shonda asked Nikki about her sex life. Nikki said, "Well, little miss nosy Shonda, if you must know, it is also ten times better. My man stays in shape and can handle all of this. Plus, he is a FREAK just like I like it."

Nikki licked her pointer finger and drew an air dot. She asked, "Now, how is your sex life? You had two men fighting over you all weekend. Which one are you going to give some, too?"

Shonda said, "I made love to Jerry this weekend, and it was great."

Everyone screamed.

Lisa said, "Shonda, I'm so happy for you."

Peace said, "My baby is growing up."

"I have been grown for a long time," Shonda said.

"Who else got some dirt to share? Jackie, what happened with you and Sexy Chocolate?" Peace asked.

"You are so nosy. Yes, we made love as well. Hell, I almost gave Stanley some, too. His arrogance was turning me on," Jackie said.

Nikki asked, "Would you go back with Stanley?"

Jackie replied, "I will always love Stanley, and never say never."

"But Jackie, you made love to Barry. Do you love Barry?" Shonda said.

She looked her straight in the eyes. "Shonda, you silly girl. I am very fond of Barry. You will see that it is easy to make love to two men if you are the one in control."

Nikki said, "Well, well. I am not the only reformed whore at the table."

Everyone screamed. "Nikki!"

Peace changed the subject. "Now that my husband has decided to run for mayor, the only way that he is going to win is with our help. So, I have come up with a name for us."

Nikki said, "Drum roll, please." The ladies beat their palms against the restaurant table.

"The Evans Way Ladies."

Okay, Peace. I see you. That is catchy. I like it," Jackie said. The other ladies nodded their heads in agreement.

"Good," Peace said. "We are going to host out first fundraiser at E's Place in six weeks. We need to raise at least $50,000. So, we can sell the little people a lot of $50 -$500 tickets, or we can do a black-tie event at $5000 -$10,000 per ticket. What do you ladies think?"

Lisa said, "We can do both, but let us start with the little people and then sell the tickets for the premier event there."

"Good idea. Is everyone okay with that?" Peace said. Everyone agreed.

Jackie asked, "Can we include Velma since her brother is a state representative and she has lots of experience in running a campaign?"

Peace said, "I don't mind, but Jackie, are you okay with it? She doesn't seem to care for you at all."

"Look, she ain't the first bitch to hate me, but you know I am a money maker. I can dance with the devil, if I have to. So yes, invite the b," Jackie said.

"Jackie, please be nice," Peace said. "

Jackie said, "Let's all, including you, Miss Holy, grab a glass of this 1787 Chateau Margaux, $250 bottle of wine. We are toasting to first, the newlyweds, Lisa and Mark. Sam and Peace becoming the mayor and first lady. Shonda and Jerry's first time making love in twenty years. Me getting some this year and wanting to give Stanley a shot, and finally my girl, my boo thing, landing a ten-carat Jean Doussett, one-of-a-kind custom diamond ring from the man of her dreams, Eric Ramsey."

Everyone said, "Cheers." They clinked their wine glasses and took a sip. The ladies then talked and laughed about events that happened on the ranch while enjoying their food.

Nikki said, "We have to wrap this up. I have to speak with my parents about my upcoming wedding. We need to set a date and discuss the who's, what's, when's, and where's."

Jackie said, "Have your parents seen the ring?"

"Apparently so, since they helped Eric design it."

Peace said, "I just ask one favor of you. Please try to wait until after the election. I can truly use your expertise with this campaign."

Nikki got up to hug and kiss Peace. "I knew that you loved me."

Jackie said, "Ladies, please do not forget Stanley's mom's service on Wednesday. I believe that it starts at 10a.m. Remember that what we discuss at our dinners stays at our dinners. Love you all. First Lady, pray us home."

Peace said, "Heavenly Father, we come to you first to just say thank you. Thank you for all that You have done for each of us. Thank You for abundance, peace, prosperity, love, happiness, and most of all, true friendship. Watch over each of our family members and provide us with safe travel. In Jesus' name. Amen."

AFTER THE FUNERAL SERVICE

Peace said, "Everything was so beautiful today. E's Place went out of the way for Mama Lewis's repast."

Jackie said, "Thank you, Peace. Eric and Nikki are really showing out big time on their events, but baby, your husband, Sam spoke just like a politician at my mother-in-law's service. Between him and Mark, it was not a dry eye in the church."

"Not only did he sound good, but my man looked good up there. And with that, I'm taking my husband home to give him his reward. Bye, Felicia!" Peace said.

Jackie said, "Nikki, where is Eric?"

"Here he is. What's up, Jackie?"

Jackie motioned for Stanley to join them. "We want to thank you two for the beautiful repast for Mama Lewis. The food, drinks, and décor were exactly what she would have wanted."

"No, Jackie. Thank Mama Lewis for caring enough about our business to support us. That means more to us than you could ever imagine. I will see you tomorrow morning at the gym. Bye, Stanley," Nikki said.

Eric said, "Yeah, man. I love you, frat. If you need anything, give your boy a call."

Stanley said quietly, "Thanks, E."

Jackie and Stanley walked to their cars. He said, "You know you are wearing that dress. I know that you wore it for me. So, I'm on my way to take it off."

She said, "Your daughters are here, and they are headed downtown. Please, no excuses."

"Whatever. Give me two hours, and I'm there," Stanley said.

The doorbell rang. Jackie looked at her phone to see if it is Stanley. She unlocked the door from her bedroom with her remote control.

Red volt candles lit up the staircase as Stanley went to her bedroom.

He opened the door to find Jackie in a red teddy surrounded by bowls of strawberries and whipped cream, and of course, two glasses of the 1787 Chateau Margaux.
"Hello, Mr. Lewis."

"Hello, Beautiful. Thank you for allowing me to come over."

"Stop the chit chat and come over and do what you came to do," Jackie said.

"With pleasure." Stanley picked up where he left off and they didn't say another word for the next two hours. They just made passionate love, Lewis-style.

———————

Jackie was running a steady pace on the treadmill when Nikki entered the gym. "Hey Boo Boo, Kitty. What's up?"

"Girl, Nikki, everything. I did it."

"You did what?"

"I made love to Stanley."

Nikki screamed so loud.

The owner of the gym said, "Hey, what the hell is with all of that noise in my upscale establishment?"

Nikki said, "Hi, Kyle. I'm so sorry."

He held up her hand. "That sorry ass, Eric, finally proposed, or is it from someone else?"

"Eric asked me to marry him while we were at the ranch," Nikki answered.

Kyle said, "You have been home for three days. Why did I have to find out this way? I better have an invite to the wedding."

Nikki said, "Of course, you do."

Kyle walked back to his office. "No more yelling."

Nikki said, "Okay. Alright, Jackie. How did it happen?"

Jackie said, "Well, it's elementary, my dear. He worked the middle."

Nikki laughed. "Oh, you got jokes. Girl, you better give me the details."

Jackie explained. "After we spoke to you and Eric, we walked to the car. He told me that I wore that dress just for him and that he was coming to take it off. So, I let him. He came over. I had the candles lit going up to the bedroom. I unlocked the doors and let him in. He came up, and it was the best sex he had given me in fifteen years."

"Damn, Jackie. What is next for you and Stanley?"

"I really don't know. But I hope he acts right at the fundraiser coming up because I am bringing Barry with me."

Nikki said, "Believe it or not, I am so happy to be officially off the market. I don't have to deal with juggling men anymore."

THE FUNDRAISER

Weeks had passed since the ranch trip. The Evans Way Ladies were in the house and in full, drama-filled effect! It's the night of the fundraiser. Peace moved around in nervous anticipation as she finalized last-minute details. The ladies worked the crowd and assisted her as well. After Nikki checked with Hector about food and drinks, she made her way toward Peace.

She said, "This is the best fundraiser ever. There are so many people dropping off checks, networking, and deal making."

"Thank you, Nikki, but you know this is only because E's Place has become the hottest place in Sterny to host an event," Peace said.

Tim joined the ladies and greeted them. "How are the wedding plans coming, Nikki?

Nikki said, "We will not start planning until after the election."

Tim said, "Okay, cool." He turned to Peace. "It is time to grab the girls for our endorsement of Sam."

Peace called all of the ladies to the stage. She said, "We would like to thank everyone that took the time to participate in our first campaign for my husband, Sam Evans. We are officially endorsing Samuel Evans, Jr. for mayor of our wonderful town, Sterny."

The balloons dropped as Sam walked to the stage. He said, "I do not know how I got so lucky to have such a beautiful group of ladies to believe in me. In life, my wife and I have had our share of ups and downs, but God pulled us through."

He wrapped his arm around Peace as Tim stood on his left and the ladies were on both sides of the couple. They flashed bright smiles as the crowd listened intently to Sam's speech.

He continued speaking. "It is no secret in this small town that I have had two children outside my marriage. I have no excuse for it. I was arrogant, selfish, and inconsiderate. However, I came to my senses really quick when my wife left me. Just like any other man that loves his wife and faced with the possibilities of losing her, I turned to my parents then to God."

Sam's words struck a chord in Stanley. He considered them as his attention shifted from his frat brother to Jackie.

Barry watched Stanley and questioned why he ever came here. Jackie was just playing him like a violin. But he had to admit, the sex was mind-blowing. Barry wasn't quite ready to let her go so easily.

Sam said, "However, it was my true friend, my pastor, Rev. Mark Taylor that guided me. I went to counseling first by myself, and then we attended together. I promised her during that time that I would never take her for granted again. Now for twenty years, I have kept that promise."

Eric stared at Nikki. He wanted to make the same promise to her. Maybe their marriage can be as a strong as Sam and Peace's.

London admired the way Shonda's dress complimented her shapely frame. Even though he imagined how he would take it off later, London started to think about how he could be a better man who also kept his promises like his main man, Sam. Hearing Sam's journey of personal change started him to think about how he could change from his immature ways. Could a leopard really change his spots, though?

However, Tim tried to keep his promise to remain a loyal campaign manager even though he couldn't fight his growing attraction to Peace. Through Sam's speech, he imagined how many positions he could bend Peace's legs. Gina attracted him, too, in her own cute, quirky way. She was eager and willing. What man wouldn't want that? Decisions, decisions, decisions. . .

Sam concluded his speech. "And as your mayor, I promise to be just as honest and put your needs first. I am a great listener who specializes in strategic planning. If you elect me, I will be here for you."

Peace led the crowd in chanting the campaign's slogan. "The Evans Way! The Evans Way! The Evans Way!"

Shonda stopped in the middle of the chant and began to feel funny. Then out of nowhere, she passed out.

The ladies screamed out. "Oh my God! Shonda! Somebody help!"

One of the guests dipped a cloth napkin into her glass of water and brought it to Peace. She lifted Shonda's head and placed it in her lap as she repeatedly wiped her face and neck.

Velma called 911, while Richard ran to the stage. He found her pulse, faint but still. The first responders entered the restaurant as Shonda was regaining consciousness.

She said, "What happened?

Richard said, "You passed out. The ambulance will take you to the hospital. I'll be right behind you, so we can run some tests."

"But I'm fine," Shonda insisted.

Richard reasoned with her. "No, you are not. People don't just pass out unless there is a reason."

London said, "I'll ride with you, Shonda."

She thanked him. As the responders placed her on the stretcher and cleared a path through the crowd, Jerry said, "No, man. Shonda is my date. Let's go."

Shonda asked the responders to stop for a minute. She asked, "How many people can ride in the back with me?"

One of them said, "Only one, ma'am." With regard to the unspoken tension brewing between Jerry and London, he said, "One can sit in the middle upfront, if you want."

Shonda said, "Jerry, will you please sit upfront? London can ride in the back with me."

Jerry gave a brief nod and stormed ahead of the responders as they directed people to move out of the way and let them through. Richard and Velma followed them.

The crowd cheered again for Sam.

Shonda yelled. "Peace and Sam, I am sorry for ruining your night."

Sam yelled back. "Do not worry. We are on our way as well."

———————

An hour later, everyone was in Shonda's room waiting to hear about her condition. The attending physician entered the room.

"I need to speak to you in private," he said to Shonda.

"Doctor, I have no secrets. You can speak in front of my friends," Shonda said as she gripped Peace's hand.

He said, "I reviewed the tests. Everything looks good." The doctor paused for a brief moment and smiled. "Shonda, you are pregnant."

What?

THE END

NEXT. . . PART 4
Jackie's Secret Life
Unwinding the Binds that Twine

www.ingramcontent.com/pod-product-compliance
Lightning Source LLC
Chambersburg PA
CBHW050756250626
47155CB00005B/2087